Tatiana's Table

Paullina Simons was born in Leningrad and emigrated to
the United States in 1973. Her bestselling novels
include *The Bronze Horseman*, *The Bridge to Holy Cross*
and *The Summer Garden*. She lives close to New York
with her husband and four children.

Visit www.AuthorTracker.co.uk
for exclusive updates on Paullina Simons.

PAULLINA SIMONS

Tatiana's Table

HARPER

Harper
An imprint of HarperCollins*Publishers*
1 London Bridge Street,
London SE1 9GF, United Kingdom

www.harpercollins.co.uk

Special overseas edition 2007

4

A Paperback Original 2007

Copyright © Timshel Books 2007

Internal artwork by Andrew Ashton © HarperCollins*Publishers* 2007

The Author asserts the moral right to
be identified as the author of this work

ISBN 978 0 00 724160 6

Set in Goudy with Americana and Caxton
by Rowland Phototypesetting Ltd,
Bury St Edmunds, Suffolk

Printed and bound in Australia by
McPherson's Printing Group

For my beloved blessed Babushka,
a wife for 72 years, a woman for 95,
my grandmother, a cook

"*Centuries of secularism have failed to transform eating into something strictly utilitarian. Food, the act of eating, is still treated with reverence. A meal is still a rite—the last natural sacrament of family and friendship, of life that is more than 'eating' or 'drinking'. To eat is something more than to maintain bodily functions.*"

ALEXANDER SCHMEMANN
"For the Life of the World"

"*Who doth ambition shun*
And loves to live i' the sun,
Seeking the food he eats,
And pleas'd with what he gets."

SHAKESPEARE,
As You Like It, II.v.[38]

Introduction

Tatiana was making lazy cabbage and the children were crowding around the pot. It made it difficult for Tatiana to stir. She had just fried the onions and was now shredding cabbage. "A little room?" she asked. But still they crowded. The girl particularly. "I'm gonna cook too, Mama. I need to see."

The boys tortured their younger sister relentlessly. "*You're* gonna cook?" said Harry, always stirring trouble. "Everything you touch you break. I feel sorry for whoever eats your cooking."

The girl hit him, he slapped her back, she squealed. Tatiana reluctantly had to intervene. "Don't make me call your father," she said. This was her standard threat but today it was a fake one, especially since today the father was not home, was not even in the country, which was the only reason Tatiana was able to make the cabbage—since he didn't eat it.

Finally they settled down—which meant they gave her a centimeter of elbow room. Tatiana was stirring and turning the cabbage. In a separate frying pan, she browned minced beef. Janie stated she didn't like cabbage. The boys said they loved it. Tatiana gave them a glance and shook her head.

"Um—Mom?"

"Yes, son?"

"Uh, what *is* cabbage?" asked Harry.

"Does Anthony like cabbage?" asked Pasha.

Tatiana's heart squeezed. Her eldest son had liked cabbage once, but she hadn't cooked it for many years. In his letters to her from Vietnam, he wrote that he ate hardly anything in Kontum but *kimchee*, the Chinese spicy cabbage. *Tell Dad, I'm eating cabbage and loving it*, Anthony wrote.

Dad read all his son's letters. He had said, "And this he is proud of? This is his little rebellion? Cabbage?"

"Yes, Pasha, Ant loves cabbage."

"Why is it lazy, Mommy?" asked Janie.

"Because it's like you."

"Mommy! Harry called me lazy!"

"Harry, stop it."

"Mommy," said Janie, "what *is* lazy?"

Around the island the children piled, sitting on bar stools and snacking after lunch. There were four of them in the kitchen that Saturday afternoon in November 1969: the youngest, Janie, who had just turned six, and two boys, Pasha and Harry. Pasha had turned eleven in August; Harry was a month away from ten. They had gone shopping earlier, helped their mother put the groceries away, and now were "helping" her with dinner. Pasha had chopped the onion—he was a pro with the chef's knife. Harry called his brother's slicing skills "frightening." Harry stirred the food as it cooked—because that's what he was, a stirrer. Janie bounced, salted, tasted, peppered, tasted, retrieved food from the fridge and wheedled for brownies with chocolate buttercream icing or cream-cheese icing or just brownies, or just chocolate.

While the lazy cabbage was cooking, Tatiana, her longish blonde hair braided, her yellow floral print cotton dress tucked beneath a pink satin apron, made buttercream icing. Harry licked the sides of the bowl (for that was his main contribution besides demanding more sugar, a request Tatiana denied), then asked, "Mom, how come you never refer to recipes? How come you're always just cooking?"

"I don't need to refer," said Tatiana. "I have it all in here." She tapped her temple.

"But you've never made this before. We don't even know what this is. And yet you're making it like you know what you're doing."

"I do know what I'm doing."

Harry skeptically snorted. He was strawberry-haired and freckled.

Pasha, blond and already significantly taller than his mother, Pasha, who was always the first one in the family to refer to a book to back up everything with concrete proof, shoved his brother and said, "Oh look at you, doubting Thomas. You've seen Mom in the kitchen, haven't you? You know she cooks and has never used books. You know how the food comes out. What are you snorting about?"

"Snort, snort," said Janie.

"You've never made lazy cabbage. Too much stuff goes in it," Harry declared. "You can't possibly remember all those ingredients and what to do with them."

Tatiana smiled. "When I bake I look. The difference between a quarter teaspoon and half a teaspoon is a difference between edible banana bread and raccoon food."

"See?" Harry turned triumphantly to his brother.

5

"See nothing," said Pasha, smacking him on the head. "You've never seen Mom look inside a book, therefore it doesn't happen."

"That's what I said! Which is why I don't believe it. Because I've never seen it."

Tatiana handed the chocolate buttercream spoon to Harry, and said, "Blessed are those who have not seen and still believe."

They watched her putter and put the bowls away, taste the lazy cabbage again, check the oven for the cupcakes. Soon they would be ready to cool and frost.

"So you want me to tell you how I learned to make lazy cabbage?" she finally said.

The children assented—but not eagerly. It was like finding out how the magician cut the bunny in half and then put the bunny back together. Some things were better left a mystery. They liked the idea of her mining the alluvial deposits but to learn her methods? They had asked, however, so it was too late. They were given.

Babushka Maya's Lazy Cabbage

Long ago, a seventeen-year-old Russian girl named Tatiana Metanova living in Leningrad went across the Neva to Dubrovka when the bridges were down to visit her Babushka Maya—her mother's mother—and said, "Babushka, tell me how to make lazy cabbage." She was just learning how to cook and wanted to make something special for someone special. Lazy cabbage was one of Babushka Maya's signature meals. Every time she made it, it came out exactly the same, exactly right, exactly delicious, and was one of Tatiana's favorites. She thought it might get to be one of Alexander's favorites, too. Babushka Maya's famous, one and only, historically passed-down, impossible to duplicate, replicate or imitate lazy cabbage.

Babushka sighed for five minutes and finally said, "So what do you want me to tell you?"

"Um, how to make it?"

"You've never cooked anything in your whole life, now suddenly you're diving headfirst into lazy cabbage?"

"Yes."

Babushka Maya widened her eyes. "Oh. I see. Yes. Of course." She nodded wisely. "I understand everything."

"No, you don't." Tatiana looked away.

"Oh, indeed I do." Babushka Maya was nearly eighty. She had lived a long life, been a painter, a cook in a Tsar's kitchen. She could no longer see out of one eye, and her hands had been crippled by arthritis. She still painted, though, still cooked. Still saw. Everything. She said with a wry, understanding smile, "I don't make it like I used to."

"I know. Tell me how you used to make it. I want to make it like you used to."

So Babushka Maya told Tatiana to get some beef, put it through the meat grinder, to chop onion, shred cabbage—

"How much?"

"How much what? I don't know. Enough to make a pot, I guess. Enough for you—and him."

Tatiana blushed.

"Enough for leftovers," finished Babushka Maya.

"But how much do you use?"

"How much do I use of what?"

"Of meat, of cabbage?"

"I use what I have. Some ground beef, a cabbage. An onion. A little rice."

"How much rice?"

"I don't know. A little. And the juice of a few crushed tomatoes, if you have them. Water. Salt. Then cover and cook. It'll be just like mine."

Tatiana painstakingly wrote down the directions. Babushka gave her two onions and one wilted tomato. Tatiana bought cabbage, one more wilted tomato, a little beef. She chopped and minced, cooked and diced, added water and crushed tomatoes, covered, cooked and salted.

When Tatiana looked inside the pot, she saw the cabbage expanding and the water decreasing. The lazy cabbage was quickly becoming a solid paste instead of a liquid stew. She turned down the heat, and added water, then went down the hall to beg another tomato from her neighbor Nina Iglenko. She added more water, but the cabbage, sponge-like, continued to expand. It absorbed as much liquid as Tatiana poured inside the pot, and grew and grew, until she had to switch to a larger pot, but still the "stew" remained thick and intransigent. At the end of two hours when it was seven o'clock and the entire family was growling with hungry frustration in the next room, Tatiana served it as it was.

Her mother refused to eat it. Which meant: she ate it and complained the whole time. Her father ate it and complained at the very end. Her sister Dasha complained at the very beginning. Her paternal grandparents kept silent, ate it, but did not ask for seconds.

Alexander ate it. He ate cheerfully, blinking at her, winking at her, and said, "No, no, it's good. It's different from what I'm used to. Slightly. But good. Really." He pushed his empty plate toward her. "Go ahead. I'll have some more."

Tatiana stormed back to Babushka Maya's across the river the following day to complain bitterly herself. Babushka Maya, sanguine and unperturbed, said, "Well, what did you do wrong?"

Lazy Cabbage

1 cabbage, shredded thin, Julienne-style, as one might shred
    a lettuce
2lb (900g) ground (minced) beef sirloin, browned in a frying
    pan with a little butter
1 onion, very finely chopped, and fried in butter until golden
1 garlic clove, very finely chopped
8oz (225g) bacon, cut up and fried till crispy and crumbled.
    (In Leningrad they used ham hock instead. Bacon was not
    easy to come by, i.e. non-existent.)
1 cup (165g) cooked white rice
4 cups (900ml) canned tomato sauce or passata
4 cups (900ml) hot, boiled water
salt and pepper, to taste
1 teaspoon sugar
Optional:
sour cream

Fry onion in a large cast-iron skillet with deep sides. Add the shredded cabbage and cook for 15–20 minutes until the cabbage softens and starts to brown slightly. Add salt and pepper to taste.

Add the bacon to the cabbage mixture, stir well to combine, add the meat, stir. Add more salt and pepper to taste, mix in a cup of cooked white rice. While this is simmering, in a separate pan heat tomato sauce and hot water, add to the cabbage, meat and rice mixture, salt to taste, add a teaspoon of sugar to cut the acidity of the tomatoes, cover, bring to boil, reduce heat to low, and simmer for half an hour or so until it's all cooked through. It should be mushy like thick stew, but not like oatmeal. If it's like oatmeal, dilute with more water. Stir in a dollop of sour cream if preferred.

Many years have passed since that first time Tatiana made lazy cabbage for Alexander. Yet it was still vivid in her mind: her grandmother's slightly hoarse, quiet voice, the taking of the tram across the river, the waning afternoon, the ache in her limping, broken leg; but above all, the desire to make something for someone, for no other reason than to please him. All this has remained, and was fresh in Tatiana's heart. Yet over time much has changed.

Some things have changed for the better: the knives are razor sharp, and the heavy pots are enamel over cast iron. The kitchen is gleaming white, not shabby, and the counters are granite. The gas stove goes on and stays on, and the ceramic dishes bake great pies. There are two freezers and a refrigerator to hold all the food that cannot be eaten this instant. There is the best white flour, the best butter, bacon and minced beef sirloin, no need for a meat grinder. There are fresh tomatoes all year round plus tomato sauce in cans, and sweet Vidalia onions. There is a food processor, a stand mixer, a handheld mixer, and plenty of mixing bowls. And, of course, Tatiana no longer has to take food into the bedrooms with her, for fear of it being stolen if left in the apartment's communal kitchen.

There is food. There is abundant bacon. That is good.

Tatiana learned the arduous way. Cooking was time consuming. Peeling potatoes, boiling them, cooling them, mincing, salting, frying them. Making batter, crusts, doughs, fillings; whisking egg whites; frying onions; simmering soup, grating cheese; kneading bread. It took time, and all in inverse proportion to the time required to eat it. The longer something took to make, the faster the people at her table ate it. She would spend three hours making *blinchiki*, and they would be gone in twenty minutes. Yes, the food disappeared from the table in an instant, in a blink, in the gulp of a drink. And yet ... the children carried the smell of their mother's kitchen with them wherever they went. The friends continued to call every weekend, asking if they could come over, bring dessert perhaps, if she would make them spaghetti, or tenderloin. Every time she was invited somewhere, she was asked to bring leek and bacon stuffing. When her daughter called from Hawaii on her honeymoon, she said, "Mommy, they had banana bread at the Four Seasons, and it wasn't nearly as good as yours. Can you make it for me when I come back?"

When given a choice between going to a restaurant and eating at home, the younger children said, "Mama cook." When they got older, it was not even a question anymore. No one went out. They all came to her house, to her table. Each morning they reached into the fridge and took out the bread she had made the night before, baked it and had warm fresh bread—sweet brioche, or croissants, or muffins. It had all started with one man, a young soldier, who had sat down at her table, but now the children, and their spouses, and their children, and the children's spouses, came to her house. They sat in her kitchen, and said thank you when she handed them a cup of coffee and a roll, said, "God, this is good. How long did it take you to make?"

"Oh," she'd say breezily, sliding the jam across the island, "this little thing? It was nothing. Like it?"

The food went in a swallow, yet the smell of brownies and blueberry pie in the kitchen lasted forever.

This is what she does now: she chooses what she knows is good, she maintains form and substance, and hopes everything else will follow. She uses only the finest ingredients; the freshest eggs, the best flour, the sweetest butter. She cooks with ground beef sirloin, the best cheese, the freshest apples, reddest tomatoes, Vidalia onions, sweet carrots, the fruitiest jam. She uses fresh lemons, fresh garlic, fresh lime, fresh oranges, quality chocolate, and half-and-half instead of milk. She hopes her end product will be better if all of its parts are good. Form and substance. She feels that way about many things in her life.

Happy eating.

CHAPTER ONE

Cooking for Alexander

The Metanovs, how they loved to eat. What a ritual it was, to sit down at the table, to drink, to have several courses, to eat until you fell joyously away, completely sated. Everybody in the family made something, everybody, that is, except Tatiana and her twin brother Pasha. He wasn't required to, and she wasn't interested. Her father's mother, Babushka Anna, prepared most family dinners. Babushka Anna had learned to cook from her mother, who had learned from her mother, and so generation after generation of Russian women passed their secrets and their recipes down to their children, who in turn taught their own children—Tatiana's father and Tatiana's aunt.

Babushka Anna cooked on stoves that wouldn't light, and in ovens that had no wood. She cooked on cast iron that was rusted and not covered by enamel, and on thin frying pans that always burned. Grumbling, she scrubbed the rust off before she lit the flame and seasoned the pan so it would rust less next time. She used not olive oil but lard. There were no refrigerators. Whatever Dasha or Mama bought they had to cook that day, unless it was winter and they could stick it on the windowsill; the irony, of course, was that in the winter there was much less food to stick on sills. They lived on the fish they caught and salted in Luga over the summer, on the cucumbers they grew and pickled, on homemade blueberry jam, on dried mushrooms, with which they made soup, and pies and small pastries. They had potatoes because Tatiana's Babushka Maya brought her own from across the river Neva. She lived in Dubrovka, and grew them on a tiny lot in her backyard. Often, people would come through her fence and steal the potatoes. She had to keep them hidden, grow them under trees and bushes. There was never much, but what there was Maya brought to her daughter's large family. It was this Babushka Maya who had had the feel for cooking, it was she who always managed, no matter what ingredients she had on hand, to make it come out all right in the end. She had the artist's approach to cooking, which was just as well, for she was an artist, a painter, and cooked as she drew—from her instinctive heart.

And this was the gift Babushka Maya passed down to her youngest granddaughter, who had been given much.

It was *not*, however, a gift that was handed to Tatiana's mother, Irina. She would rather have mopped the kitchen floors, cleaned bathrooms, washed clothes, stood in line for three hours than make food. Throughout her adolescence, Tatiana was convinced she was walking in her mother's footsteps. Her sister Dasha, and Babushka Anna, and her twin brother Pasha, and her father all mocked her. "Tania," they would say, "how are you ever going to get married?

What is your poor husband going to do? When he comes home and asks what's for dinner, what are you going to tell him?"

"I'm going to tell him, go wash up, darling, I've got six cooks in that kitchen."

And they would laugh. "Now *that's* a way to keep a husband."

"There are women who don't cook," Tatiana defended.

"Name us one."

Tatiana wanted to name her mother, but didn't, out of respect. Because Mama did cook a little bit. What Tatiana wanted to articulate and couldn't was that Mama didn't *want* to cook. Her grandfather, whom she called Dedushka, was her sole defender. "Leave the girl alone. When it's time, she'll learn. The time has obviously not come."

But Tatiana was certain: I will be like Mama. I will cook, but I will never like it.

And she might have continued in this fashion, and perhaps indeed become like her mother, who cleaned and sewed and ironed and kept the family train crankily running. But a thing happened that Tatiana hadn't counted on.

She fell in love.

She still didn't know how to cook, but when she broke her leg and couldn't work, she had to start to help her family, and little by little she did, with failed starts and meager attempts. She felt herself to be useless, and thought that not only would Alexander not love her after eating her food, but might actually grow to detest her when he saw just how hopeless she was.

And yet he came when he could and sat at her table, smiled at her, said, "So, what's for dinner tonight? Don't tell me. Put it on my plate and let me guess."

She would put it on his plate. "Hmm," he'd say, chewing and contemplating. "Fish sticks?"

"No! It's hamburgers with zucchini."

"Oh. Yes, also good."

But his eyes twinkled.

Just as she was learning how to love, food became more scarce, then disappeared altogether. Still Tatiana tried to cook to give her family life. She toasted crusts of bread, made oatmeal with water, chicken soup without chicken, simmered beans and barley. Every once in a while, when Babushka Maya brought a few potatoes from Dubrovka, she cooked them as best she could, and when there was no more heat to cook with, she cut them up and the family ate them raw, then ate the peelings. Tatiana sliced her daily ration of cardboard bread, and ate the damp, shrivelled chicory beans they had used to make ersatz coffee on the *bourzhuika*, a little wood-stove, and dreamed of a time when she could cook and Alexander would eat her food and rejoice in it.

The man she fell in love with was from a different world. But Tatiana often felt that she too was from a different world. She felt in many ways she thought herself to be slightly apart from her friends, from her cousin Marina, from her family. She didn't know what it was about herself that was different and kept these thoughts to herself, tried to keep herself to herself. She didn't want other people to notice her eccentricities.

But when she met Alexander Belov that summer day in June, Tatiana wordlessly felt that he was a soul also slightly apart, and yet a soul not apart from her. He was familiar in both tangible and intangible ways, but also as alien from her guileless, innocent understanding as a man could be and still remain part of the same species.

He was born Alexander Barrington in Barrington, Massachusetts, United States of America, on 29 May 1919, the day of a full solar eclipse when the moon completely obscured the sun. This day of his birth was significant for other reasons in the history of mankind. It was on this day, an ocean away, a man by the name of Arthur Eddington of the Royal Astronomical Society in Greenwich, England, was photographing this solar eclipse under which Alexander came into the world to once and for all test a certain theory by a certain clerk in a Swiss Patent Office by the name of Albert Einstein.

Einstein speculated that space and time were not absolutes but rather relative to their position to other objects and relative to the speed at which the objects were traveling. If the test failed and the sun's rays did not bend as Einstein had postulated, Einstein said his theory of relativity would be false. If the test showed that the sun's rays traveled at twice the speed Einstein predicted, the theory would also be false. At 1:30 p.m. on 29 May 1919, Eddington took sixteen photographs of the earth moving out from the shadow of the moon. At 6:30 p.m., three thousand miles away, Alexander came into the world.

And before Tatiana and Pasha were born in 1924—what a year to be born! Lenin dying, Stalin taking power—before her sister, Dasha, was born in 1917—what a year to be born! the Tsar abdicating, one Party coming to power, unrest, a putsch, a coalition of parties vying for power, a violent revolution—before all that, Tatiana's dutiful, diligent, morose mother Irina was born in 1898 to a thirty-eight-year-old woman named Maya and her husband Fyodor. Maya was the Tsar's cook, and Fyodor the Tsar's Praetorian guard, stationed at Pavlov Barracks. Fyodor served three tsars and in the spring of 1904 left for Japan, leaving behind his wife and seven-year-old daughter, his only child. He never returned. Maya waited for him a long time. Since she never received a telegram regarding his fate, she continued to believe that perhaps he was having a hard time making his way back to her.

A decade passed. Then another. And another.

Maya lived carrying the hope in her heart that her Fyodor was just around the corner, and might any minute be back. She never remarried. "How could I?" she would say to Tania when she asked why the wonderful Uncle Misha never became Maya's legal husband. "I think there is a law against that, no? I'm already married." No talk of divorce on the grounds of abandonment would sway her, and when she died in the winter of 1941, she died not Fyodor's widow but his wife.

When younger, Maya had liked to read Lermontov, the unabashed romantic of the Russian poets. She, a young woman in St. Petersburg, an artist, a painter, waited a long time for love. Her friends were married and had had children ten years before her, but yet she waited, despite being petite, charming and sought after. She waited for the man her own mother would have approved of. When she met Fyodor, who was five years her junior, she knew, despite the scandalousness of the age difference, that she had found that man.

Maya's mother, Liza Prisvetskaya died young at fifty-one when Maya was twenty, and she always maintained that her mother had died of a broken heart. Although the official cause of death was heart failure, Maya would declare, "Like I said, a broken heart." Maya had loved her mother, who taught her how to sew, how to read poetry—and how to cook. Everything Maya knew about how to be a good woman she had learned from her mother, who in turn had learned it from her mother.

Liza Prisvetskaya's mother, Milla, was in her own day the pastry chef's assistant at the royal court. When Milla was barely seventeen, she fell in love with a man who was in love with another woman— his wife. But this man's wife, Natalya Goncharova, treated her husband terribly. A poet, he needed to stay home to do his work, but Natalya, much younger than he, loved parties and dancing, loved the attention of male eyes and male hands. She would frequently leave her husband home to write his poetry, which she considered a silly and melancholy endeavor, while she gallivanted around the numerous St. Petersburg balls by herself. At one of these occasions, she began an inappropriate dalliance with a middle-aged man named George D'Anthes, quite a few years older than she. Rumors of their flirtation reached the ears of the poet, as he was writing his great masterpiece. Crazed with jealousy, he confronted his wife, who denied all charges, called her husband irrational, then pledged her love. But her nocturnes continued, undimmed by conjugal responsibility. Natalya persistently denied her husband's accusations, even though, as a joke, St. Petersburg high society made him a member of the "Petersburg Society of Cuckolds," unbeknownst to him but beknownst to everyone else, including Milla.

Enraged and confused, the husband began going out on his own to reclaim what remained of his pride, of his good name. Paradoxically, to do so he gambled and drank. At one of the gambling clubs he frequented, he met Milla, Liza's mother, Maya's grandmother, Irina's great-grandmother, and Tatiana's great-great grandmother. The romance, if there was one, was secret and short-lived. Secret because Milla was engaged to marry one of the poet's gambling-club partners. Short-lived because the poet, at the end of his rope and unable to bear the terrible things that were being said about his wife, challenged George D'Anthes to a duel. On an icy February morning in 1837, the poet met with George D'Anthes in a deserted St. Petersburg field. D'Anthes fired first, gravely wounding the poet, who fired second, only to superficially wound D'Anthes.

The poet died later that night.

George D'Anthes was expelled from Russia, never to return. He died in exile in 1895, and never saw Natalya Goncharova again. The poet was secretly buried in a monastery by Tsar Nicholas I himself, because he was afraid of having a revolution on his hands if the residents of the city found out where their beloved poet laureate was being put to rest and how ignominious had been his end.

The poet was Aleksandr Pushkin. The narrative poem he wrote in the months before his death was "The Bronze Horseman." It was the last thing he wrote.

Meanwhile, Milla married her career civil servant and gave birth to a child, Liza, on 12 October 1837, nine months after Pushkin's death. And though Milla never mentioned Aleksandr Pushkin to anyone, dying herself just four years later of tuberculosis, there were whispered rumors—never proven and never corroborated since both witnesses to the truth were now dead—that Liza Prisvetskaya was Pushkin's child. After Milla's death, the rumors quietened down and then vanished altogether, for it was evil to speak ill of the dead. Milla's death ensured that the truth was buried with her. But she did pass her beauty onward, and she did teach her daughter Liza who taught her daughter Maya who taught her daughter Irina who taught her daughter Tatiana the secrets of pastry, pies, pelmeni, and poetry.

Beef Stroganoff

Tatiana made this only once for Alexander in Leningrad because by the time she was learning to cook, the meat was nearly gone. She managed to buy half a kilo of pale-looking, fatty beef and stretched it for ten people by adding noodles, mushrooms and a little sour cream. There wasn't enough sour cream, not enough butter, not enough noodles, or meat, or even mushrooms. Only onions were abundant. Alexander ate the Stroganoff, and continued asking for it even when meat was long gone, and then noodles, and soon even onions. But still he persisted, a joke on pale par with the piece of beef he now longed for.

"Alexander," Tatiana kept saying, "why do you ask for this? You know we have no meat. Are you joking with me?"

"Not joking, torturing you, Tania," Dasha said in her philosophical, no-nonsense tone.

"Someday, Tania," Alexander said, "I'd like to have Beef Stroganoff again."

"And someday you will," interrupted Dasha, "if my sister doesn't kill you first!"

They said nothing, Tatiana and Alexander. He lit a cigarette and busied himself with the small oven. She went to fetch water in a pail so they could have tea. But what she prayed for was this: Please. Someday let me make Beef Stroganoff for Alexander.

   1lb (450g) sirloin steak, rib-eye, or shell steak
   ¾ cup (110g) all-purpose, (plain) flour
   2 teaspoons salt
   1 teaspoon pepper
   4 tablespoons (50g) butter
   1 large onion, thinly sliced
   8oz (225g) button mushrooms
   1lb (450g) fettuccine, cooked, drained, and buttered
   8oz (225g) sour cream

Trim the fat off the steak and slice into ½-in (1cm) thick strips 2–3 inches (5–7.5cm) long.

In a medium bowl, combine flour with salt and pepper, mix thoroughly, then add the steak, coating each piece. Use more flour/salt/pepper mixture if need be.

In a large skillet, on medium-high heat, melt 2 tablespoons of butter, add onion, cook until golden. Add another tablespoon of butter, and the mushrooms, cook until mushrooms are golden. Add the rest of the butter, and the steak, and continue cooking on medium-high, turning occasionally, about 10–12 minutes. When the meat is cooked through, turn off the heat, and stir in the sour cream. Adjust the seasoning as necessary. Salt is usually needed. Serve over the buttered fettuccine. The Russians served it with wide egg noodles, or vermicelli, which are tiny egg noodles. *Lapsha*, they called it. But not much *lapsha* in Russia in 1941 . . . 1942 . . . 1943 . . .

Meat Cutlets with Onions

Cutlets sounds fancy in English. Something extra special with meat, which was also pretty special, since it was so hard to come by. But really, meat "cutlets," or *Kotlety* in Russian, was just another name for hamburgers, with eggs, breadcrumbs and onions. *Meat* was what made these special. "We're having *meat* cutlets!" meant someone was in the shopping district, saw a line, stood in line for forty-five minutes, possibly ninety, and got lucky enough to buy beef when they got to the counter.

Tatiana found out, during her seventy-eight-day sojourn in Stockholm, that in Scandinavia, these were made smaller, rolled into little balls and called Swedish meatballs. But the recipe was almost identical, except the Swedes served it with lingonberry jam and cream gravy. Tatiana liked it that way, too. Having meat again after so many years was one of her few joys in Stockholm.

To eat it like the Russians do—serve the meat cutlets with boiled new potatoes tossed in dill and butter, or with egg noodles, or with mashed potatoes. If you want to do like the Americans, serve in hamburger buns, with French Fries on the side. What's good about the recipe is that it's multi-centric and multi-cultural while unchanging in its essence.

2½lb (1.15kg) ground beef sirloin
1 medium onion, grated or very finely chopped
1 large garlic clove, grated or very finely chopped
2 eggs, lightly beaten
3 slices bread, pulped for a few seconds in a food processor,
    for fresh breadcrumbs, or ⅔ cup (85g) store-bought
    breadcrumbs
2–3 ice cubes, or ¼ cup (55ml) ice water
salt and pepper, to taste

In a medium bowl, combine all ingredients and mash together, either with a masher or with your hands. But be forewarned, hands will be numb, as the beef and the ice are quite, umm, icy. Shape into large ovoid balls, slightly smaller than tennis balls. Flatten them if you wish; Tania's mother did not, but in the U.S. because they like to put the burgers between buns, flattening them makes them easier to eat. Shallow fry on medium-high heat for 7 minutes on each side until golden brown.

Pelmeni

Pelmeni was everyone's favorite winter food, next to *blini*. Who wouldn't like meat wrapped in a small fistful of dough, frozen, then dropped into boiling chicken bouillon and served with butter and sour cream?

Tatiana knew who didn't like pelmeni. The person who had to make pelmeni. And that would be Babushka.

Babushka Anna would rather stand in line for three hours in winter to buy pelmeni at the store than make it herself. As she would say, "*Slishkom mnogo vozni.*" "Too much effort."

But her family loved it. And so Babushka, groaning and sighing, creaking and complaining, getting an impatient Dasha to help her, made pelmeni.

A food processor would have made things easier—the mincing of the beef, chicken, veal. The kneading of the dough. But there was no food processor. A freezer would have definitely made things easier. There wasn't one. And since pelmeni needed to be frozen and kept frozen, it could only be made in the winter. The little dough balls were placed on metal sheets and put on the windowsill, with the window left slightly open so they could freeze, and after that, were collected into bags and left on the ledge.

They were made in the communal kitchen, and as soon as the rest of the residents in the apartment found out someone was making pelmeni, they would creep out of their rooms, ingratiating themselves in hope of receiving a little of the final product. Babushka would say, "Help me fill the dough rounds and I'll let you have some when they're done." That's when the neighbors started to haggle. "But Anna Lvovna, why should we stand at the table for thirty minutes making the pelmeni with you, when all you're giving us is thirty? We've got a family of six!" or "How about I get to take all the pelmeni I make? I make two, I take two. I make a hundred, I take a hundred." "Yes, yes, we know you supplied the meat, but you're not being reasonable. Yes, yes, we know you stood in line for one hour to buy it, but meat or no meat, without our help, there would be no pelmeni. Don't be stingy. You can't ask for help and then refuse. You can't offer pelmeni and then not give enough for one lousy dinner. Look how many you have. It's just not right, it's not comrade-like, Comrade Metanova."

So Babushka would make them, all the while saying this was the "absolute last time" she was *ever* making pelmeni.

In Arizona, thirty years later, there was slightly less hassle. The freezers had plenty of room all year around, the kitchen was large, the island at which to stand and make the dough balls ample, the cookie sheets abundant, there was music playing, the sun shining, and the food processor did much of the prep work. One thing the food processor could not do: corral children who wanted to be swimming, chasing jackrabbits, shooting baskets, working in the shed with their dad, into the kitchen to help their mother cut out the dough rounds, spoon meat filling into them, and seal the edges. When they were younger, the boys' argument against helping was, "Why do we have to do it? Dad never helps you. If it's such a great job, why doesn't Dad help? I don't see him sealing meat balls. He'd rather clear brush."

The father, who could not, in this one instance, lead by example,

would order his errant sons to help their mother, allowing no argu-
ments. Every once in a while, he tried to help her himself, and he
got a little credit for that, but his hands were too big; he couldn't
seal the pelmeni properly, nor could he put a small enough amount
of meat into them. His version was to make not 500 small balls, but
ten large ones, like pies you then boiled in water. And Tatiana,
grumbling and shaking her head, lamenting how many things
remained the same despite others changing so dramatically, would
make the pelmeni herself, in honor of her cranky and under-
appreciated grandmother.

The standard recipe makes ninety pelmeni. An adult can eat
twenty, a child ten. So if you have a family of five, all that fuss is for
one dinner. Tatiana recommends making more. When she decides to
make them, she makes 400–500 to store in her freezer and remem-
bers fondly the few pelmeni-bags laid out on her window-sill in
Leningrad, freezing under the December blizzard winds.

Pelmeni:

To make the dough:

6 cups (750g) all-purpose (plain) flour
2 teaspoons salt
6 egg yolks
1 cup (225ml) ice water

Combine flour and salt in the bowl of a food processor. Pulse for 2 seconds. Change to continuous mode and with the blade running, add eggs yolks and ice water. Process until dough collects in a ball on the blade. Cover with plastic wrap (cling-film) and let rest for 30 minutes at room temperature.

Filling:

1lb (450g) ground beef sirloin
8oz (225g) ground chicken
8oz (225g) ground veal
1 large onion, very finely chopped
salt and freshly ground pepper, to taste
1 cup (225ml) ice water

While the dough is resting, make the filling in two batches (because one probably won't fit). Combine half the meats in the bowl of a food processor and pulse until thoroughly ground. Add half the onion, salt and pepper and pulse until fully processed. Add half the water and pulse again until smooth and fluffy. Transfer to a large bowl and repeat with the other half.

To assemble the pelmeni:

On a floured surface, roll out a chunk of dough, about a quarter of the total, into a large circle approximately 18 in (45cm) round. Make the circle no thicker than $\frac{1}{16}$ in

(1.5mm). Cut out rounds about 2½ in (6cm) in diameter with a knife or cookie (biscuit) cutter. Gather the remains of the dough, roll out again, and cut more circles.

Spoon about a teaspoon of meat mixture onto one half of the round, brush the edges of the dough with one slightly beaten egg white (so that it sticks together better). Fold over the other half to make a semi-circle, pinch tightly closed with your fingers. Fold the edge over itself to make sure it's sealed shut.

Arrange the pelmeni on a baking sheet or plate, making sure they're not touching. Freeze. Repeat with another ball of dough. And another. And another.

Once the pelmeni in the freezer are solid, transfer them into freezer bags, seal tightly and keep frozen.

To cook pelmeni:

Bring to boil 1–2 cups (225–450ml) of liquid for each serving. Add 1 chicken bouillon cube per cup of liquid. When the water boils add the requisite number of pelmeni, 20 for adults, 10 for kids, turn the heat down to simmer. Stir once or twice to prevent sticking. Pelmeni is ready when it floats.

Serve in the broth with a little sour cream and spicy mustard on the side. If you prefer pelmeni without the soup, ladle into a bowl, add a little butter, and serve with sour cream, mustard, or horseradish on the side. The Russians like all three at once.

Papa's Borscht

Papa, Tatiana's father, didn't cook much. He had too many women around him to cook himself—his wife, his mother, his sister, his oldest daughter. But there was one thing he made because as he said, "Women cannot do this right." He made borscht, a very hearty soup indeed. He said borscht was a man's soup. He cooked the beets raw, right in the broth, but added three tablespoons of vinegar, without which they lost their red color. He would say to his son, "Pasha, come see how a man makes borscht." But Pasha wasn't interested. Papa didn't ask Tatiana to come; he knew she wouldn't. Dasha was the only one who would come. "Papa, can I watch you?" Papa would sigh and mutter about his impossible younger children, and knowing that Dasha already knew how to make the soup, he would nevertheless tell her, "Women cannot make borscht. Just ask your mother."

Tatiana would think to herself that Mama wasn't a particularly fair culinary example of what women could and could not do.

She thought, when I grow up and have my own family, I will make this soup for them, and it will be as good as Papa's. And when she lived in New York, she did make it a few times for her little family of two, plus her best friend, but that was the last time Tatiana ever made borscht. Perhaps she would have appreciated it more had she known she would not make the soup again. She was left instead with a sorrowful nod of the head at her relentless memory, as if she were answering her long gone father. "Indeed Papa, indeed. No one makes this soup like you."

1lb (450g) beef chuck or other stewing steak, cut into 1-in
  (2.5cm) cubes
1lb (450g) beef marrow bone
1lb (450g) pork spare ribs
2 large onions, 1 peeled and left whole, 1 coarsely chopped
½ cabbage
3 garlic cloves, very finely chopped or grated
3 carrots, coarsely chopped
3 large cooked beets (beetroot), cubed
16oz (450g) canned peeled whole tomatoes
3 potatoes, peeled and cut into ½-in (1cm) cubes
2 tablespoons butter
3 tablespoons tomato paste
salt and pepper, to taste

Garnish:

fresh dill
sour cream

   Place beef chuck, marrow bone, spare ribs, whole onion and
garlic into a large, preferably cast-iron over enamel, 9-quart
(8.1-liter) pot. Add 2 quarts (1.8 liters) water, salt, pepper,
bring to boil, then lower heat and cook, partially covered, for
an hour or more until meat is tender. Meanwhile in a frying
pan in 2 tablespoons butter on medium heat, sauté chopped
onion and cabbage until softened and golden, and add to the
stock. Add the can of peeled tomatoes and the tomato paste,

stirring gently until the paste dissolves. Add carrots, beets and potatoes to the stock. Continue cooking for another 45 minutes, until vegetables are tender. Serve with chopped fresh dill and sour cream.

Mama's Mushroom Barley Soup

Tatiana's mother made her favorite version of this soup, and Tania considered herself lucky that it was Pasha's favorite too, because Mama made it much more often since he liked it. Pasha was Mama's favorite child and though Tatiana felt competitive with him over many things, if his favored status got her her beloved mushroom barley soup more often, then she considered that a personal victory over him. Without opening her mouth, she got what she wanted. Of course, Pasha, being the most contrary and obstructive of brothers, after discovering Tatiana's affection for "his" soup, would deny himself the pleasure of having it as long as he denied her the pleasure of having it, too. That was his victory over her. And so it went.

Tatiana wheedled her mother into preparing this soup for Alexander. There wasn't another opportunity to make it for him again until much later, in another life. In that life, Alexander liked the soup and ate it, but said it reminded him of impossible things. Not just of Russia, of not having meat, of winter, as if that alone weren't plenty. No, it also reminded him of sitting wet under the Polish trees in the mountains of Holy Cross with a young captain, when they had no food and couldn't cook it if they had, for then the Germans would smell fire and food, and sniff out their position. So instead the two men talked about mushroom barley soup, and whether Tania still liked it, and wondered if at that very moment she perhaps was eating it hot out of a big bowl, somewhere else in time, somewhere safe, where there was food enough, and fire.

After Alexander told her this, Tatiana cooked it less often. When she did, though, they both sat and ate in silence. Sometimes she poured it into one large round bowl, gave them each a spoon and they would eat, quietly, their heads leaning together.

Tatiana's grandmother made this soup with whole peppercorns instead of freshly ground pepper, and Tatiana ate it like that until she came to the United States and started making it herself. She became convinced that her grandmother had been slightly sadistic because the peppercorns permeated every spoonful and once you bit into one, you couldn't taste anything else. Tatiana heartily recommends skipping the Russian self-inflicted pain-in-the-mouth tradition and grinding the pepper.

2oz (50g) mixed dried mushrooms
1 large onion, minced (very finely chopped)
2 tablespoons butter
1 bay leaf
salt and freshly ground pepper, to taste
5 cups (1.125 liters) cold water plus the mushroom water
3 large potatoes, peeled and cubed
3 large carrots, peeled and cubed
½ cup (100g) pearl barley
sour cream, to serve

Rinse the dried mushrooms in a colander to clean off the grit and sand. Then soak for 4 hours in 1 cup (225ml) cold water. When the mushrooms feel soft to the touch, drain, and pat dry. Reserve the soaking water for the soup.

In a large heavy saucepan cook the onion on medium-high heat in 2 tablespoons butter until soft and slightly golden. Add mushrooms, cook for 5 minutes. Add the soaking water, the 5 cups of clean cold water, the bay leaf, salt and freshly ground pepper and bring to boil. Turn down the heat, cover, and simmer for 45 minutes. Add potatoes, carrots, and barley, bring to boil, turn down the heat, and cook another 45 minutes, or until the carrots are tender and the barley soft. Serve with a spoonful of sour cream.

Salad Olivier

Dasha was very good at peeling potatoes, and Tatiana said this was why Salad Olivier was her favorite food—because it was made of the one thing Dasha was really good at preparing.

To this Dasha replied that for someone who did not even know how to peel potatoes, it was an ironic mocking indeed, but this observation increased rather than stopped the derision.

There is no Russian get-together, celebration, feast, party without this salad. This salad and the next are *de rigueur* in Russian cuisine.

6 large cooked potatoes, cooled, peeled and finely cubed
6 hard-boiled eggs, (p.105), cooled, peeled and very finely
   chopped
1 yellow or red onion, very finely chopped
1lb (450g) bologna or similar cured sausage, finely diced
6 medium pickles or better yet, cucumbers in brine (salty
   pickles), squeezed dry with a paper towel and finely
   diced
5–6 tablespoons mayonnaise
salt and pepper, to taste
16oz (450g) canned peas, drained

Place the first 5 ingredients in a large bowl, then add the mayo and mix carefully. Finally, add the peas, mix *very* carefully, so as not to mash them, and refrigerate for a few hours before eating to let the flavors seep through. Eat for lunch, or as an appetizer before dinner, but be warned, the salad is very filling. Perhaps a bowl of soup with some bread would be a sufficient accompaniment.

Venigret

Like all Russians, Tatiana loved beets. And as venigret is for beet lovers, it is, therefore, for all Russians. And they love this salad because no matter what else there isn't much of, there are usually plenty of beets. You can always dig up a root vegetable somewhere in the Russian soil. Which is why beets, potatoes and onions are a staple of Russian cooking. This was something Tatiana *could* have made in Leningrad—it was certainly easy enough—but she didn't. Despite not making it, though, she knew *how* to make it, and in New York, prepared it twice a month for a tall black-haired beauty who had never had beets before, all the while mourning a tall black-haired man who had loved them.

6 cold cooked potatoes, peeled and finely cubed
6–7 cold cooked beets (beetroot), peeled and finely cubed
1 small onion, very finely chopped
6 pickles or cucumbers in brine, squeezed dry and finely chopped
3 tablespoons sauerkraut, drained
salt and pepper, to taste
3–5 tablespoons olive oil
1 16-oz (450g) can cooked peas, drained

Add ingredients in order, peas last, being careful not to mash them. Chill for a few hours to allow the flavors to develop.

Blini, or yeast-risen pancakes

Maybe caviar is an acquired taste, but *blini*, thin, crêpe-like pancakes risen on yeast, are the royalty of pancakes and *not* an acquired taste. They are the perfect complement to black or red caviar. Both were generally available in Russia.

And during Butterweek, the Communist equivalent of Lent but without the fast, God, Easter or salvation, Russians feasted on *blini* with caviar, with sour cream or butter.

Blini were not cooked in summer, and the most Tatiana could do during that first summer when she met Alexander was to wish for winter to arrive so he could come in from the cold in his coat and hat to have *blini* with caviar because they seemed to her to be just the kind of food he would love. She would learn to cook them by the time winter came, and he would eat them and be pleased with her. And while she was right about his feeling for *blini*, she was wrong about wishing for winter to come.

2 teaspoons dried yeast
4 teaspoons sugar
3 tablespoons warm water
1 egg, beaten
3 tablespoons butter, melted and cooled to room temperature, plus extra softened butter for frying
2 cups (450ml) milk
2 cups (250g) all-purpose (plain) flour
1 tablespoon vegetable oil
½ teaspoon salt

Prove the yeast. In a cup, stir together yeast, one teaspoon of sugar, and warm water and let stand 5–10 minutes until frothy. In the bowl of a stand mixer beat egg, butter, and the rest of the sugar and the salt. Then, alternating milk and flour, beat on low setting until smooth and thick, the consistency of heavy cream. Add yeast, beat until smooth. Add butter and oil and continue beating. Make sure batter is smooth. Cover and let stand in a dark, preferably warm place to let the batter rise, 45 minutes to an hour. Stir, let stand another 30 minutes. Stir well. Pancakes are now ready to be cooked.

Preheat an 8-in (20cm) non-stick pan on medium, butter the pan. Pour in half a ladleful of batter, swish around to just cover the bottom and cook about 30 seconds. Pancakes should be thin, like French crêpes. When bubbles form and break on top, flip with a spatula and continue cooking for another 15 seconds or so, then turn out into a buttered oven-proof dish. Don't cover the dish, otherwise the *blini* will get soggy, but place into a 250°F (120°C) preheated oven to keep warm. Cook the rest of the *blini*, which should take no more than 45 seconds each.

CHAPTER TWO

Leningrad

The river sparkled at night when the light filtered in rays of hope
with golden sunlight glinting streaming across the midnight waters,
and Tatiana touched the rough speckled granite with her hand and
it was cool to her touch, and as she bent over the wide ledge she
saw in the water the reflection of the golden spire and knew that
for an instant, before the next siren, warning of the Luftwaffe bombs,
she was at peace.

The Metanovs lived life loudly and to the full, though not always
peaceably. They yelled, boisterously recollected, drank, put on their
shoes, crowding in the narrow hallway, threw on their coats, grumbling, and rumbled down the corridor, lighting cigarettes, tying up
scarves, elbowing the aunt and uncle who came to visit, pinching
the cousin, pulling the fraternal hair. So loud, so crowded, so glori-
ously alive.

And as they lived, they ate. When there was meat, they cooked it, and when there was sugar, they baked with it. They made bread and buttery desserts, and poured cream over layers of flaky dough, piled blueberry jam onto their plates. They drank heavy black tea with lots of sugar, and it was good, and the pancakes and *blinchiki* were good. They bought black caviar by the kilo from Yelisey gastronome store on Nevsky Prospekt, and fried their thin, crêpe-like pancakes called *blini* in butter, had sour cream, hard-boiled eggs and onions as condiments on the side. Even in the village of Luga, on the shores of a river where meat was scarce, they happily ate the fish freshly caught that day. They caught the fish early in the morning or late at night and fried or boiled it, simmering the heads for soup on a Primus stove lit by kerosene. They had cucumbers from the gardens, eggs from the chickens and drank warm milk to bursting morning and night. Instead of butter they rubbed sunflower oil and salt on their black bread. They thought they had so much, had it good, all things considered. And they were right, for all too soon came 1941 and Hitler, war and winter.

Then, even dried stale bread toasted in the oven was a luxury. The Metanovs called them toast points, and ate them without caviar, without butter, without oil.

Fade, fade. Little by little they all faded.

Only one small Metanova girl remained, carrying in her soul the soups and salads, the blueberry pancakes and cabbage pies; carrying them with her to distant continents far away from the white-night canals and the troubadours, oceans carrying them away from the four-story pastel-green building built in the 1800s with the plumbing to prove it. Away from the Luftwaffe bombs. Through frozen Karelian marshes and iced-over Bothnian gulfs, through Scandinavian ports and across the North Sea she came, crawling on her belly to another world, carrying the old world within her.

Continents and oceans took long to traverse, but what separated Tatiana from the place where she once lived with her family and the place she lived now, was the blink of an eye. Blink, and there they are. As if there is just a swinging door between them. She can hear the arguing and yelling, hear the boisterous clean-up, the fiery discussions around a small table, glass falling, and laughter. The difference was: she lived. And as it turned out, that made all the difference.

The boy they had made in the old world came with her into the new, carrying on his little shoulders the weight of generations of Metanovs and Barringtons. The recipes came with her. And something else too: the inextinguishable love she felt for one man.

Together out of the ashes of despair, Tatiana and Alexander's son clawed out a new life, tried to build another family of just two where once there had been twenty. And in this life, in time, the old recipes were supplanted by the new. Tatiana carried Russia inside her, but other immigrants carried Italy, Indochina, and India. Thus, next to meat *pirozhki* in her repertoire appeared a risotto and curry, and later sauces from Naples and challah bread from Germany.

The poetry came with her, too, words painted like rivers by Osip Mandelshtam and Anna Akhmatova. *I've come back to my city*, wrote Mandelshtam, eight years before he was silenced for good. *These are my own old tears, my own little veins, the swollen glands of my childhood . . .*

And Akhmatova, Leningrad's poet laureate, prayed in verse:

41

*O Lord, help me to live through this night—I'm in terror for my life,
your slave: To live in Petersburg is to sleep in a grave.*

Bread

The bread of life. Flour, water, salt, sugar; milk, eggs, yeast, butter.
A complete food, bread.

"Darling, what can I make you?"

"I'm full, Tania."

"You haven't eaten since lunch. You must be hungry."

"Lunch was barely two hours ago, and we've had a kilo of blueberries since then."

"Maybe some tomatoes with bread?"

"No, thank you."

"I have some cold potatoes from yesterday. I can make salad
Olivier—well, salad Olivier without the eggs. Or the kolbasa. Or
pickles. Or peas. Just a little potato salad with onion—and a piece
of bread?"

"Funny, but no, thank you."

"Some blueberry jam with bread?"

"I'm sick to *death* of blueberries."

"I have salted fish. Would you like some fish between two hunks
of bread?"

"Tatia . . ."

"Some cucumbers with tomatoes and onions and salt? With black
bread?"

"Come here."

She came.

He draped his big arms around her, pulling her down on his lap. "I will have," Alexander said, "a big hunk of black bread, dipped in sunflower oil and rubbed with salt." He didn't let her jump up. "I will get it. Okay? You sit, you jumping bean. I'll be right back."

Tatiana sat and waited for him on the bench, a moment, two. Then got up and went inside the hut after him. The door closed behind her.

The bread of life. Oat flour, linseed oil. Water, glue, cardboard. A complete food, bread. Take, eat.

She tried to scrape off the ice with her nail so she could see out the window, it was noon and there was a bit of sunshine now. If only she could scrape off the ice, some of the hour-long daylight would filter through the pane. Her nail broke as she tried. Not just the top of her nail, no, her whole nail slid off her finger as if it were nothing but a piece of loose skin. There wasn't even blood in its place. She studied it in the dim light. My body is falling off me, she thought. There will be nothing left for him when he comes back next. If he comes back next.

She reminisced of the years before, the late thirties, when there was flour, milk, and yeast, all taken for granted as she lived, went to school and ran around in Luga. They ate bread and never thought about it, almost like breathing, and suddenly here they were, thinking about something so fundamental as bread. They made all sorts of deals with themselves as people in despair do. Please, if you give me bread now, I promise I'll never take it for granted again. I'll never leave a crumb of food on my plate, I'll never take more than I can eat, I'll treasure bread, every hunk of it, just . . . give me some now. Please. I'm hungry. Feed me. Please.

Who were they praying to in the blizzard days of 1941? Who were they hoping would intercede on their behalf? Many of them never prayed. This just goes to show you, they said. This is what we always believed, and this just proves it. We are all alone, as we suspected. Look what's happening to us in this godless world.

Still they dreamed of a better life where they could make bread and rejoice in it. Please, o Lord, feed me.

"Dasha," Tatiana said. "Why is there something so comforting about bread?"

"This bread?" Dasha couldn't believe it. "This isn't bread."

"No, not *this* bread. That's not what I'm talking about."

"So what are you talking about?" Dasha was in no mood to discuss the various merits and demerits. She was soundlessly counting down from a hundred, three times in a row, before she allowed herself to give in and have the last piece of her sawdust bread at five o'clock in the evening, instead of at seven.

Tatiana stopped talking. There was something about bread that transcended cultures and values and time. This became clear only when the bread was gone. From bagels and brioches, crumpets and croissants, from sourdough bread and French baguettes, to won-tons and dumplings—not to mention sweet pastries, pies and pancakes.

To go without was unthinkable.

And yet, here they were. Without.

"Let's eat the bread, Dasha," said Tatiana.

44

"It's not even five."

"I know. I'll get more tomorrow morning. Or maybe Alexander will come back late tonight, bring us something. Let's eat."

She broke the cube of bread, the size of half a deck of cards, broke it in half, then in quarters, and bowed her head. A complete food, bread. Flour, water, salt, sugar; milk, eggs, yeast, butter. A complete food, bread.

Yeast Dough for Crusty White Bread:

Butter, for greasing
3 teaspoons dried yeast
7 teaspoons sugar
3 tablespoons warm water
4 cups (500g) all-purpose (plain) flour, sifted or 3¾ cups
   (450g) bread flour, sifted, about a pound of flour
1 teaspoon salt
1¼ cups (275ml) milk, boiled and cooled to warm
2 eggs
⅓ cup (75g) unsalted butter, melted and cooled to warm

Glaze:

1 egg yolk
1 tablespoon melted butter

Butter a mixing bowl.

Prove the yeast: stir it with ½ teaspoon sugar and 3 table-spoons warm water in a small cup and place under heat lamp for 10 minutes, or let stand in bowl of warm water for 10–15 minutes.

Meanwhile, in the bowl of an electric mixer, combine the flour, salt, and remaining sugar, then add the risen yeast and the warm milk, and beat with the standard beater attach-ment for 1–2 minutes on low. Add the eggs and beat for 1 minute more. Add the butter and continue to beat for another minute on low, then change the attachment to a dough hook and beat on medium for 10 minutes until the dough is smooth and comes off the beater as soon as you turn it off. Remove from the bowl and knead by hand 3–4 times. If it peels easily off your hands, it's ready to rise. If it's still sticky, put back in the bowl, and beat for 2 minutes more, or knead by hand for 3–4 minutes, and test again.

Roll the dough in the buttered dish so that it's coated with butter on all sides. Cover with a clean dish towel (tea towel), and let rise in a dark, warm place (80°F/27°C) for an hour until doubled in size. Lift the dough 1 foot out of the bowl and let it fall. Repeat. Then re-cover and let rise again for a half hour in the same place, until doubled in size.

On a floured board, roll out the dough with your hands to elongate it. Cut into thirds. Roll each piece with your hands until it resembles a rope about 15–18 in (37.5–45cm) long. Attach the three strands of dough at the top by twisting them slightly, then braid the rest, and twist-tie the bottom the same way as the top. Cover and let rise another hour. Preheat oven to 350°F (180°C). Grease a cookie sheet.

Prepare a glaze: 1 egg yolk, a tablespoon of melted butter, a tablespoon of water. Mix well.

Uncover the bread, place on prepared cookie sheet, brush with glaze, let stand a couple of minutes, and bake for 40 minutes until the bread is rich golden in color. Let cool for 30 minutes before slicing.

That is what Tatiana dreamed of in darkness. But this is what she made:

Toast Points:

She took the scraps from stale bread and toasted them for two hours in a 250°F (120°C) oven until the bread was all dried out. When it cooled, she transferred the toast into canvas bags, tied them and kept them in a safe place, allowing her family to take one or two scraps from the bag after all the other bread was gone and all the rye flour was gone.

Soon the toast points were gone, too.

Other bread products she dreamed about while down on the floor breathing in the heady fumes of dried toast: pie crusts, *pirozhki* pastry, shortbread pastry. Others: pancakes, thin, thick, buttermilk. Dumplings: bread filled with meat and boiled. And still others: cookies, Napoleons. Then the king of them all: bread pudding— just bread, bread, and more bread covered with butter and milk, sugar and eggs. The antithesis to the blockade, to the siege, to war, to toast points. Too much of all the good things. But mostly, bread.

Cabbage Pie

When making this, prepare the dough with one hand while holding a copy of Aleksandr Pushkin's book of poetry in the other. The pie just won't taste the same without Pushkin's conflicted contemplations on sacrifice and civilization in his epic poem, "The Bronze Horseman".

The first time Tatiana made cabbage pie, in August 1941, she made it without a copy of Pushkin's book. She was too busy trying to add enough onion to the meat to fill one pie to feed her hungry family. There wasn't enough. She had to barter with the woman next door, a suspicious sort who always thought Tatiana was up to no good. But she managed to convince Zhanna to give her a cabbage, for which Tatiana would give her a quarter of the finished pie. So, that evening she made her meat pie mostly with cabbage. Cabbage, onions, and a little meat. It was good. It was all gone. What they didn't know then: that was the last meat and the last cabbage the Metanovs would lay their eyes on.

In the dead of winter, saved by a diminished but unvanquished Alexander, Tatiana had managed to claw her way out of Leningrad, out to the Ural Mountains. And under unrestrained bombing, spring came to a diminished but unvanquished Leningrad. It was too late for the Metanovs, but this time, the other Leningraders prepared for the worst. What if the blockade wasn't broken by next winter? Onions, potatoes, turnips, cabbage were hearty things that grew with ease in the earth. The citizens planted them in the shallow squares and gardens in the middle of their city, and along their canals and rivers and next winter, when the blockade was still not broken, they had more food.

And in Lazarevo, their place in the sun, there was cabbage, and marriage, and Alexander was content to eat the pie his young wife made him, teasingly lamenting her lack of interest in fishing. He would have preferred stuffed cabbage, the unlazy brother of lazy cabbage, but stuffed cabbage required it be stuffed with something like meat, and there was none. Or rice. So instead they ate Tatiana's cabbage pie by the banks of the Kama River, quoted Pushkin to each other, argued about his not-so-hidden meanings, and privately dreamt of an impossible future, where perhaps cabbage with meat might be possible.

Little did they know that the impossible future indeed would come, in another life, but with two people so changed, that though he ate meat, he could never touch cabbage again despite being given a second chance at life, and she, though she ate everything, could not stop trudging to a hospital fifty hours a week to heal the unhealed, to save the unsaved.

Pie Crust 1

This is an all-purpose pie crust, good for places where there is refrigeration. So if you live in a place where there's refrigeration, this one's for you.

The key is cold butter, cold shortening, cold egg, ice water. Because we have creature comforts like Ziploc bags, you can chill the flour mixed with the salt in a Ziploc bag. To make the butter as cold as possible, cube it and put it in the freezer for an hour before adding to the flour.

During the coldest Leningrad winters, Tatiana's grandmother made this recipe by hand without a refrigerator. She put the butter and the flour on the windowsill to freeze. And, as she had no Ziploc bags, she used wax paper.

This will be enough for two round 9-in (23cm) pie crusts.

3 cups (400g) all-purpose (plain) flour plus extra for dusting
½ teaspoon salt
½ teaspoon baking powder
2 sticks (225g) unsalted butter, frozen, plus extra, unfrozen, for greasing
2 tablespoons shortening, chilled
1 egg, cold (you can omit the egg if you wish. The Russians like the egg.)
½ cup (125ml) ice water
3 teaspoons cider vinegar

Place flour and salt inside bowl of food processor. Take the butter out of the freezer and shortening out of the fridge, slice with a sharp knife, add to the flour, and pulse for 10–20 seconds, until the butter mixes with the flour and looks like small ground peas *or* coarse oatmeal. Beat the cold egg and add to the mix. Add ¼ cup (55ml) ice water and pulse again for a few seconds, until mixture becomes more like pastry, and forms a solid ball. Add the rest of the ice water and the vinegar, and pulse for a few seconds more until all the water and egg is absorbed and the dough holds together. Don't overpulse, you'll toughen the dough. On a cool, lightly floured surface, divide the dough in two and form two flat cakes, like thick plates or shot putter discs. Cover each with plastic wrap (clingfilm) and refrigerate at least 2 hours.

Pie Crust 2

Though there was no ice water or Western-style shortening, this is the one Tatiana made in Lazarevo when she made cabbage pie for Alexander. She used lard. She placed flour into a bowl, made a cavity in the center, dropped the lard inside, and chopped it with two knives. When the dough was crumbly, she added cold water from the river, mixed, and then formed the dough into two balls, wrapped them and placed on a window sill in the early morning when it was cold. The food processor and a freezer takes out the guesswork, and shortening greatly improves the quality of the pastry, but the point is, you can make it by hand too, if you live in a remote summer village with no refrigeration and want your beloved to be your friend.

2 cups (250g) all-purpose (plain) flour
2 sticks (225g) shortening, chilled
½ cup (125ml) ice water

Pulse flour and margarine in a food processor until just crumbly. Place this mixture in a large bowl, add ice water and use a pastry blender to form a dough. Don't use your hands, they'll warm the dough. When the ice water has been blended through, form into a ball, cover with plastic wrap and refrigerate as long as possible, preferably overnight.

Cabbage Pie Filling:

4–5 tablespoons butter, plus extra for greasing
1 onion, finely chopped
1 cabbage, shredded
salt and pepper, to taste
1 cup (165g) cooked white rice if you have it.

By all means, if you have meat, include 1 cup cooked and salted ground sirloin. And it goes without saying, if you have bacon, add crisp-fried and chopped-up bacon.

Melt butter in a large heavy-bottom frying pan. Add onion,

cook on medium till golden. Add cabbage, turn up heat to medium-high, cook until cabbage softens. Reduce heat, continue sautéing for 10–15 minutes, stirring frequently, until cabbage is fried golden and soft. Add rice, meat or bacon if you're using it, mix, cook for a few minutes, turn off the heat.

For the pie:

butter, for greasing
flour, for dusting

Glaze:

1 egg yolk
1 tablespoon melted butter
2 tablespoons water

Preheat the oven to 425°F (220°C). Grease and flour a 9-in (23cm) pie dish. Take one disc of pie crust 1 out of the fridge, roll out on a lightly floured surface into a 12-in (30cm) round, and press into the prepared pie dish. Pile the cabbage filling into the pastry, heaping it slightly in the middle. Roll out the other half of the pastry into a 12-in (30cm) round. Cover the pie and press tightly all around with your fingers to seal the edges. Brush with a yolk/butter/water glaze. Cut a 2-in (5cm) cross in the middle, place on the bottom oven rack, and bake for 45 minutes until golden brown on top. Serve with soup.

Mushroom Pie

"Oh, Babushka, what are you making?" Tatiana squealed.

"What does it look like?" Babushka Anna barked, sweaty and frustrated with her task.

Tatiana looked. There were mushrooms and onions in the pot. It could be any one of a dozen things. She had to be careful not to undermine Babushka's efforts. She could say one wrong word and . . .

"My favorite—mushroom *pirozhki?*" Bite-sized pies with meat.

"*Pirozhki?* In the summertime? You've lost your mind!"

"Alexander and Dimitri are coming to dinner," Tatiana said. "They'd love some *pirozhki.*"

"This is not a restaurant. They'll eat what they're given and be grateful for it. You want to stand here two hours and help me make *pirozhki?* Ah. I didn't think so. Now leave my kitchen and stop bothering me. Help your mother set for dinner."

Sighing, Tatiana left, noting that she had not gotten an answer to her simple question: "Babushka, what are you making?"

Not *pirozhki,* that was for sure.

Mushroom Pirog (Pie)

Use Pie Crust 1 or 2. See p.50/51.

Mushroom Filling

2½ lb (1.15kg) fresh mushrooms
2 large yellow or brown onions, very finely chopped
3 garlic cloves, very finely chopped
2 slices rye bread with or without caraway seeds, or 1 cup
  (165g) cooked white rice. Or both.
salt and pepper, to taste
oil and butter, for frying
Optional:
3–6 tablespoons very finely chopped fresh dill. (Dill has a
  strong taste. If you love it like the Russians do, by all
  means use it.)

Glaze:

1 egg yolk
1 tablespoon melted butter
2 tablespoons water

Wash the mushrooms thoroughly. Pat them dry and chop
finely. Sauté in an oil and butter mixture, in four batches so
they don't steam. Place mushrooms in mixing bowl while

you sauté the onions in a little butter until golden. Add garlic, sauté for 20–30 seconds more. Return mushrooms to the frying pan, reduce heat and cook for another 5–7 minutes until the liquid has evaporated. Take off heat, cool slightly. Your pirog is now ready to be assembled.

Remove the crusts from the rye bread and pulse bread in a food processor until it forms fine crumbs. In a medium bowl combine the breadcrumbs, cooked white rice and the mushroom mixture. Mix well.

Preheat oven to 400°F (200°C). Grease a cookie sheet.

On a floured board roll out the dough into a rectangle 13 × 18 in (32.5×45cm). Place onto the cookie sheet. Arrange the mushroom mixture lengthwise down the middle of the pastry. Fold the edges over the top, and seal well, moistening your fingers with milk and pressing the seal closed. Brush with the yolk, butter and water glaze. Bake for 40–50 minutes until golden.

Pirozhki

Pirozhki: little balls of yeast dough wrapped around a meat filling and baked in an oven until golden and crispy.

Many times, Babushka Anna tried to teach Tania how to make these *pirozhki* before the war, before even any intimation of war. To say Tatiana had no interest would be like saying a pine tree had no interest. Her curiosity extended only to science experiments. If she put in three cups of flour instead of two, what would happen to the *pirozhki?* If she put in four cups of sugar instead of one, what would happen to the dough? What about if she made the filling with just onion? Onion *pirozhki!* Now that was funny to Tatiana. No one else thought so. She got sent to bed, Babushka and Dasha made the *pirozhki*, and another year passed, and another. And then war came.

And now the sisters were lying in bed under the covers, whispering, shivering, waiting for Alexander to come. There was no heat, no light, no food. Everyone else was gone.

"Tania, what are *you* suddenly so upset about? Like *you* have anything to be upset about. What's wrong with you?"

Tatiana was mouthing the words, trying to get them out, trying to find the voice.

"What?"

"Dasha . . . why didn't I learn how to make *pirozhki* when Babushka tried to teach me?"

"Because you didn't care."

"That's right. But now she's gone, and I don't know how to make it."

"Tania, I hate to point out the obvious," said Dasha, "but I think we have bigger problems than you not knowing how to make *pirozhki*."

"A minute ago you said I had nothing to worry about."

"Certainly not this!"

"Tell me how to make it, Dashenka, *milaya*," whispered Tatiana.

"That's what you want to talk about? Making *pirozhki?* Pastry with meat?"

"What do *you* want to talk about?"

And as heavily as she could muster under the scratchy woolen blankets, Dasha sighed and rolled her head from side to side to show her exasperation at her impossible sister.

Pirozhki

Yeast Dough Pastry:

2 teaspoons dried yeast
4 teaspoons sugar
⅔ cup (150ml) lukewarm milk
1 cup (225g) butter, melted and cooled to room temperature
1 egg, beaten
3½ cups (450g) all-purpose (plain) flour
¾ teaspoon salt (if you're using salted butter, reduce salt to ½
  teaspoon)

Combine yeast and sugar in a large bowl, blend in milk, let stand 5–10 minutes until frothy.

Pour in butter and egg, beat with a wooden spoon.

Sift in flour in several batches, stir well. Knead dough for at least 10 minutes on a floured surface until soft and smooth. At first it will be lumpy. Keep going. Get comfortable, look at it as great exercise for your arms and knead away until it becomes like elastic.

Shape into a ball, cover lightly, let stand in a dark place 15–90 minutes. You don't have to let it rise for 90 minutes. It'll taste great even after 15 minutes of rising. You can make the dough first and while it's rising, prepare your filling. But, if the dark place you choose is the inside of your oven, *don't* forget to remove the dough before preheating the oven to

425°F (220°C). (Tatiana says this as someone who speaks from bitter experience.) You can make the *pirozhki* either with a mushroom filling (recipe below), or with the meat filling on p.64.

It's hard to go wrong with this pastry recipe; it's forgiving of all mistakes.

Mushroom Filling:

2oz (570g) fresh mushrooms
1 large yellow or brown onion, very finely chopped
1 garlic clove, very finely chopped
1 slice rye bread
½ cup (80g) cooked white rice
salt and pepper, to taste
oil and butter, for frying
Optional:
4 tablespoons very finely chopped dill

Glaze:

1 egg yolk
1 tablespoon melted butter
2 tablespoons water

Wash the mushrooms thoroughly. Pat dry, and chop finely. Sauté in an oil and butter mixture, in four batches to let the steam evaporate. Set aside while you sauté the onions in a little butter until golden. Add garlic, sauté for 20–30 seconds more. Return mushrooms to the frying pan, reduce heat and cook for another 5–7 minutes until the liquid is gone. Take off heat, cool slightly.

Remove the crusts from the rye bread and pulse bread in a food processor until it forms fine crumbs. In a medium bowl combine the breadcrumbs, cooked white rice and the mushroom mixture. Mix well.

While nearly a pound of flour sounds like a lot it's not really that much. This recipe will make you two cookie sheets of *pirozhki*, if you make them small, possibly sixty in all.

Preheat oven to 425°F (220°C). Lightly grease cookie sheets. Break dough into pieces, roll thinly, cut with a cookie (biscuit) cutter or with a glass into 2½in (6cm) rounds. Spoon a teaspoon of filling on one-half of the round, brush the inside with a little milk, fold over, pinch with your fingers to close tightly, or use a fork dipped in milk. Arrange on the cookie sheets. In a small bowl, combine an egg yolk, 2 tablespoons water, and 1 tablespoon melted butter, and brush the *pirozhki* with the yolk glaze. It will make the *pirozhki* golden, shiny and buttery. Bake 17 minutes, check after 15. Enjoy. With soup. To warm up, you can wrap the *pirozhki* in a paper towel and nuke (microwave) for 10–15 seconds per *pirozhok* (singular); be careful not to overheat, easy to do. The microwave will make the dough soft.

Blinchiki

Babushka Anna was not as patient as Babushka Maya, that is to say, not at all. In July of 1941 she was making soup after standing in line for beef bone and being lucky enough to get one with some meat on it.

Tatiana walked into the kitchen, but she wasn't bubbly tonight. "Are you making *blinchiki*, Babushka?" she asked tiredly.

"I might, sunshine. If you help me, I might. What say you?"

"I think I'll be fine with just the soup," said Tatiana.

"I'm not asking you to make them, God forbid, Tatiana Metanova!" boomed Babushka. "Just to help me."

Oh, how Tatiana regretted asking. To come into the kitchen and to ask the cook what she was making, why that was simple politeness. To walk by would have been rude. And yet . . .

Anton, her friend, had asked her to go to the roof tonight. She had just worked ten hours at Kirov, making flamethrowers; she still smelled of nitroglycerin. She had also walked four kilometers with Alexander by her side before he finally saw she was exhausted and they caught a tram back home.

"Okay," said Tatiana. "What do you want me to do?" It was said in the tone of one saying, "Would you like me to pick up these twenty bricks and walk twenty kilometers with them in bare feet over rusty nails?"

"That's the spirit," said Babushka. "First, let's make the batter. Because it's got to rest while we make the meat filling."

"OK." She wished she could rest.

"Go get me some rice." "Can you take the meat off the bone and put it through the meat grinder?" "Can you chop an onion?" "Tatiana! What are you doing? You're holding that knife as if you've never chopped an onion before."

"Um—I've never chopped an onion before."

"Oh, for God's sake! Here. Give me that."

Tatiana gave her that—gladly. She boiled some eggs, watched the water boil, and the rice simmer. She ground the meat, twice—both times badly. Anton was already on the roof. She hadn't even changed from work yet. And was she mistaken, or did Alexander, as he was reaching over to grab the strap on the tram, let his hand slow down as it was traveling past her hair? It almost seemed like he was—

"Tania! Are you paying attention? Look—the rice is burning at the bottom. You had one thing to do, and you can't even watch the rice?"

Tatiana tried to separate the eggs but couldn't, running through three precious eggs in the process. Babushka's loud imprecations made it impossible for Tatiana to daydream effectively, but when her hands were dry, she did touch the back of her head, to see how her hair might feel to someone who perhaps wanted to linger on it a moment or two.

When they were making the thin pancakes, Tatiana was unable to flip them over. They were too thin. They kept breaking.

"Tatiana." Her grandmother spoke slowly, as if controlling the imminent implosion. "We have enough batter for twenty-four *blinchiki*. No more, no less. If you ruin three *blinchiki*, we will only make twenty-one. Who's going to have three fewer *blinchiki* because your head is in the clouds?"

"I guess me, Babushka."

After they cooked the pancakes, Tatiana had to assemble them, put meat filling inside each one and fold it over. That took another half hour.

"Are we done?" she said. She was too tired now even for day-dreaming.

"Go away," said Babushka. "I still have to fry them. You go away. I can see you're not up to this. Go set the table."

Tatiana went, set the table. But by the time the *blinchiki* were ready, just fifteen minutes later, she had fallen asleep, in all her clothes, on top of her bed. No one woke her, and the next morning when she got up to go to work, all the *blinchiki* were gone.

I will never make these as long as I live, Tatiana said to herself. I'd rather make bullets and tanks all day.

But they were her favorite food. They were everyone's favorite comfort food. *Blini* without yeast: French crêpes into which you spoon a meat filling, traditionally made to accompany beef bouillon, with ground meat from the soup.

To make *blinchiki* is a labor of love. To make twenty-four takes Tatiana two hours. If Tatiana is also making soup, or doubling the recipe, it takes even longer. *Blinchiki* are a special-occasion-only king of meals. But maybe worth it if you're trying to get the man you love to love you back, or perhaps if you want to tell him you're pregnant. Or perhaps when your firstborn child is nominated to become Chairman for the Joint Chiefs of Staff. Make them once, feed your family, and then decide if they're worth it.

Blinchiki:

The Batter:

(for 24)

2 eggs, separated
½ teaspoon salt
½ teaspoon sugar
2 tablespoons unsalted butter, melted
3 cups (675ml) milk
2 cups (250g) all-purpose (plain) flour

In a stand mixer, process the yolks with the salt and sugar. Then beat in the butter. Alternate adding the flour and milk to the batter, then leave the mixer on for 10 minutes. This makes the batter very smooth, like heavy cream, and the *blinchiki* come out tender when cooked. Cover and let rest for an hour while you prepare the meat filling, or your soup, or both.

The Meat Filling: (also use for pirozhki *with meat)*

1 cup (165g) cooked white rice, add a little extra butter to the rice
2 hard-boiled eggs, cooled
1 large onion, coarsely chopped
1¼lb (570g) ground beef sirloin

salt and pepper, to taste
A couple of teaspoons of chicken stock if you have it on hand, or light cream if you don't, or both if you feel like it. It's all good.

In a large frying pan, fry the onion on medium-high in a little butter until lightly golden. Add the ground beef, fry on medium-high, until cooked through. Lower heat. Add salt and pepper to taste. Add the cooked rice, mix thoroughly, continue cooking on low, for 5–10 more minutes, adjust seasonings.

In two batches, add the meat filling into the bowl of your food processor fitted with a standard blade, add the chicken stock and/or light cream, add the eggs one at a time, replace cover and pulse carefully, maybe 3–4 times. Do not over-pulse, or you will be eating pâté on crackers instead of a chunky, uniform meat filling.

To make the blinchiki *crêpes:*

Preheat an 8-in (20cm) *non-stick* frying pan on medium, grease with a little butter. Tatiana learned how to grease her pans from the Russians—they cut a raw potato in half, dip the potato in a little melted butter and rub it over the pan. This method greases the pan just enough and no more.

Pour a small ladleful of batter into the pan and swirl around to spread evenly. Cook for 30 seconds or so. Flip the pancake and cook for 10–15 seconds, until just barely set, then lightly and carefully slide out onto a wooden board, the more cooked side *up*.

Grease and pour another ladleful onto the frying pan. While the second pancake is cooking, assemble the one on the wooden board. Put a tablespoonful of filling in the middle and fold it over four times like a present. Place the assembled *blinchik* (singular) on a cookie sheet lined with aluminum foil or wax paper. Don't forget about your cooking pancake. It's ready to be turned out.

Continue in this fashion, until all the *blinchiki* are cooked and assembled.

One caveat: be careful not to talk, to turn away from the stove, to get a drink, to yell at the kids, to use the facilities, to change the CD in the player, and especially not to answer the phone. There is not a second for mistakes, and no extra batter to spare. You've slaved over a hot stove too long and too hard to chat with your girlfriends now. Don't think you can leave the frying pan empty while you attend to your other life either. If you leave the pan empty, it will get too hot and burn your next pancake. If you turn it off, it will get too cold and your next pancake will be glue. Perfection demands attention.

You're almost done. After the *blinchiki* are on cookie sheets like little packages, get out a few more frying pans, and prepare to fry the *blinchiki*. Heat the pans to medium, perhaps even medium-high, for 2–3 minutes. Add a few tablespoons butter. Make sure the butter sizzles but does not burn; the *blinchiki* will taste horrible cooked in burned butter. If this should happen wipe the pans clean and start again. Fill the pans with the *blinchiki*, and cook for a minute until golden and crisp on the bottom. Brush a little melted butter on top of each one right before you flip them over so the topside can get golden crisp. Flip, lower the heat, and cook for 2–3 minutes longer.

Set your crisp golden *blinchiki* on large plates and serve immediately, with soup or with a light tomato and cucumber salad, and a little sour cream on the side if you wish. *Tak vkysno!* So delicious!

What's for dessert?

Babushka Maya's Russian Napoleon

"You know what I feel like right now?" The girls were lying in their bed, staring up at the ceiling. It was night.

"What?" It was winter.

"Napoleon. Babushka's Napoleon. God, it's so delicious. That's what I want." There was snow outside. A moon perhaps—or flares from rockets? The flash of blue light reflected the snow into the windows, allowed them to see the contours of things: dressers, chairs, cracks in the ceiling, barely breathing mouths.

"Did you hear me, Dasha? I feel like Napoleon."

Dasha paused. She was mulling. Silent. Then she said, "Funny, but you don't look like Napoleon."

"Oh, hah. Tell me how to make it."

"I told you last week."

"Tell me again."

Sigh. "It's so delicious, isn't it, but such a fuss to make," said Dasha. "Six layers of flaky dough with pastry cream in between. So much work. Babushka made it only on New Year's."

"If it had been up to her, she would have cooked only on New Year's. Babushka thought everything was such a fuss to make. Every single thing."

"Easy for you to say. You never made anything."

Tataina had to defend herself. "I cooked some things in August."

"You call that cooking?" But Dasha said that mildly. She had no fight in her. "You were always such a naughty girl." It was said with tenderness. "Every New Year's Babushka made Napoleon and would put it covered on the dining table for the cream to soak through, you would tip-toe down in the night, and eat a dozen squares, readjusting it so no one would notice."

"If no one noticed, then why did you holler at me?"

"Well, you did eat a third of the family Napoleon all by yourself!"

"It was so good."

"Yes." They fell silent. "What day do you think it is?" Dasha asked.

"I don't know. Late December sometime."

"Yes, but when?"

"I don't know. Very late December. Why do you ask?"

"I'm wondering if New Year's is coming up. New Year's Eve, 1941."

Tatiana stared at the ceiling, as if expecting to find the answers there. "You want some Napoleon, Dasha?" she whispered.

"Yes, Tanechka. It's a good dessert to make for a feast, to celebrate. Alexander used to like sweet things."

"Yes," said Tatiana, still staring upward. "Maybe we already missed it."

Napoleon:

Pastry Dough:

4 sticks (450g) unsalted butter, softened
1lb (450g) all-purpose (plain) flour
2 tablespoons fresh lemon juice, chilled
¼ cup (55ml) ice water
3 large egg yolks

Cream the softened butter for 1–2 minutes in an electric mixer. Add flour and beat on low speed for 1–2 minutes. Add lemon juice and ice water to the mixture. Add egg yolks. Replace beater with a dough hook, and beat for 2–3 minutes on medium. Shape into a large ball, cover with plastic wrap (clingfilm) and refrigerate for at least an hour. While it's refrigerating, make the custard.

For the custard cream filling:

1 quart (900ml) half-and-half, or 1 part cream and 2 parts milk
2 vanilla beans, split lengthwise, seeds scraped out
7 egg yolks

1 ¼ cups (250g) sugar

5 tablespoons butter, plus 8 more tablespoons

5 tablespoons all-purpose (plain) flour

¼ cup (50g) butter

1 tablespoon vanilla extract

Heat the half-and-half with the vanilla beans and their seeds until bubbles just start to form. Take off heat, let stand while the half-and-half infuses with the vanilla.

Meanwhile, in an electric mixer with the balloon attachment beat the yolks and sugar for 10 minutes. Turn the speed to low. Remove the vanilla beans from the half-and-half and slowly add the liquid to the egg mixture. Or stir in with a hand-held whisk, until fully blended.

In a 3-quart (2.7-liter) saucepan, melt 5 tablespoons of butter and add the flour, stirring constantly for 3–4 minutes until it forms a roux paste. Slowly add the custard, stirring constantly on medium-low heat, until the mixture comes to a boil. Custard will be thick by now. Simmer for a minute or two, stirring occasionally, then take off heat. When it's cooled down to about 170°F (77°C), add the remaining 8 tablespoons of butter stirring until fully melted. Add vanilla extract, stir, cool, and refrigerate before use.

To assemble the Napoleon:

Preheat oven to 375°F (190°C). Separate dough into 6 even-sized balls, cover each one, and refrigerate those you're not using. On a floured board, roll out one ball into a rectangle about 9 × 13 in (23 × 32.5cm) and ⅛ in (3mm) thick. Bake on an ungreased cookie sheet for 10 minutes until pale yellow. Do not overbake. Remove to a piece of wax paper, let cool. Continue in this way until all six layers are baked, stacking them one on top of another, separated by wax paper.

Reserve one for crumbling on top of the Napoleon. Take the best, strongest layer, place it on a rectangular board covered with wax paper, and with a spatula spread a layer of cream on top. Place another pastry layer on top, spread with more cream. Continue until all the cream is gone and five layers are used. Crumble the sixth layer into small crumbs, and sprinkle on top of the cake. Refrigerate for at least 4 hours, preferably overnight, so the pastry has a chance to absorb some of the cream. Keep refrigerated. It keeps and cuts very well, and is wonderful with morning coffee. Or tea, like the Russians do.

Potatoes with Mushrooms

Just like that, from one life to another. Barely even a breath. Just a struggle, a collapsed lung, tuberculosis, a nighttime burial, and unconsciousness for four months. Then suddenly, it's spring again, and there is a little black bread, the cows are giving milk, there are fish in the water and canned pickles from the summer before. Soon there will be potatoes. When it rains there are mushrooms in the woods, and with some fried onion she can make something hearty, like potatoes and mushrooms. Then one more breath, and a grimy man in an officer's uniform with a rifle slung on his back walks incongruously down the dusty road, looking for her in Lazarevo.

And there is only breathlessness between running to him and standing in a church, waiting for the priest to marry them. The iconostas is in front of her. The church smells of incense. It's quiet, not even her breathing breaks the silence. All that echoes in her heart, besides dread fear for the future, are his words. *"Tatiana, will you marry me? Will you be my wife?"*

"I'm hungry," he whispers, before the priest arrives.

"You're always hungry," she whispers back.

"Isn't that the truth." He tries to keep his expression even, but his pupils dilate, his eyes dance. He leans to her. Blushing she tries not to lean away.

"When we get back, can you make potatoes with mushrooms? I love how you make it."

Dasha used to make this dish for Tatiana in Luga when there was nothing else to eat, no fish, no cabbage pie. Tatiana's heart continues to hurt. "Hmm. We'll have to go into the woods to pick the mushrooms." The priest arrives at last to marry them.

Alexander straightens up. "Perhaps another time. We won't be picking mushrooms tonight."

6 tablespoons butter
6 tablespoons canola oil
1 medium onion, cut into paper-thin strips
8oz (225g) mushrooms, sliced

6 medium potatoes, peeled and cut into thin strips, about ⅛ in
(3mm) thick
salt and pepper, to taste
Optional:
½ cup (125 ml) sour cream, or half-and-half

In a large skillet, on medium-high, heat 1 tablespoon butter and 1 tablespoon canola oil, add the onion, cook until golden. Add 1 more tablespoon butter and 1 tablespoon oil, when butter melts, add the mushrooms and cook until these too are golden. Add the rest of the butter and oil, and when butter melts, add the potatoes, mix thoroughly with the onions and mushrooms. Lower heat to medium, and cook, turning occasionally so the potatoes don't burn on the bottom, until cooked through and soft. If you like your potatoes crunchy, add a little more butter and oil and turn up the heat. If you like them a little softer, turn the heat down to medium-low and partially cover. Serve with sour cream if you want to be like the Russians.

Tatiana's Buttermilk Pancakes with Grated Apple

"Shura! I need your help."

Alexander drops his axe, comes to stand near her. He had been chopping wood. There is a bowl between her legs, egg whites in the bowl, a fork in her hand. "What do you need?"

"I need you to whip these egg whites to a fluffy stiffness."

"Um—why?" He takes the bowl and fork from her.

"Because." She stands up. He sits down. "There is no pancake recipe on earth that some whipped-up egg whites cannot make better."

He starts mixing the eggs slowly with the fork. "Who told you this?"

Dasha had taught her this, as she had taught her many things. Tatiana doesn't answer him. "Shura, faster. I can do it slow myself. I need your strength. You have to do it really, really fast."

"Why?"

"Otherwise they won't get fluffy. I wish I had a proper beater. Faster!"

He is moving the fork in circles as fast as he can. After five seconds he stops. "It's not working." The egg whites are still runny and translucent.

"Where's the Red Army endurance? Three to five minutes!"

"Three to five minutes? Are you kidding me? I don't do anything for three to five minutes."

She stares at him. He stares at her. The fork falls to the ground.

"Shura, no! Breakfast! Pancakes!"

She runs away. He chases her.

When he catches her near the shoreline and lifts her into the air, she tries to persuade him. "Shura, listen to me."

"I'm listening." He kisses her neck.

"Flour, buttermilk, sugar, fluffy egg whites. Yum, right?"

"Yum, yes." He kisses her face.

"With grated apple. Buttermilk pancakes with grated apple."

"Sounds very good." He kisses her lips.
"Shura . . ."
"Yes?"

1 egg yolk, plus 2 egg whites
2 tablespoons sugar
½ teaspoon salt
4 tablespoons butter, melted and cooled, plus extra for greasing
2 cups (450ml) buttermilk
2 cups (300g) flour (Tatiana has only buckwheat flour. By all
    means use white instead.)
1 teaspoon vanilla extract, or fresh lemon juice
1 apple—Granny Smith or Cortland are best
maple syrup, to serve

Preheat the oven to 200°F (100°C). In the bowl of an electric mixer beat the egg yolk with the sugar and salt. Add the butter, then alternating amounts of buttermilk and flour.

Grate one apple, mix through. Add vanilla or lemon juice.

In a medium bowl, whip the egg whites until fluffy, fold carefully into the batter. It's now ready to be cooked.

Preheat griddle or shallow frying pan on medium, grease with butter. Drop small ladle fuls of batter onto the griddle, leaving a 2in (5 cm) space between them. Cook a minute on one side, flip over, cook 15–30 seconds on the other.

Transfer the pancakes to an ovenproof dish and place in the preheated oven. Continue cooking the rest of the pancakes.

Serve with warm maple syrup.

Alexander and Tatiana didn't have any maple syrup. They didn't mind. He dreamed of syrup from the sugar maples of New England, and she dreamed of bananas that she'd never tasted, but wished she could put into her buttermilk pancakes. "Served with warm maple syrup," added Alexander.

Blueberry pie

In Russia they had Granny Smith apples, which made the best apple pie. Sometimes, if the export market had been good, the Metanovs stood in line to buy Red Delicious. Softer apples, like Macintosh make the worst pie—too soggy, like mashed apples. There were no Macintosh apples in the Soviet Union.

Tatiana preferred blueberry which took no cinnamon at all—of which there was little, and certainly none in Lazarevo—but lemon juice, zest, sugar, cornstarch and a tiny bit of salt. Alexander was sick of blueberries. Tatiana could tell because every time she made anything with blueberries—blueberry pie, blueberry pancakes, blueberry jam, he said, "I'm sick to death of blueberries."

"Well, I have no apples."

"Oh, fine, let's have blueberry. But apple pie would have been nice. Apple pie with a little cinnamon."

Use Pie Crust 1 (see p. 50.)

The Filling:

4 cups (570g) fresh blueberries, stems removed
2 tablespoons fresh lemon juice
1 teaspoon lemon zest
½ cup (100g) sugar
2 tablespoons cornstarch (cornflour)
⅛ teaspoon salt

Roll out one pastry disc into a 12-in (30cm) diameter ring. Line a greased and floured pie dish with it, cover with plastic wrap (clingfilm), and refrigerate while you make the filling.

Set a pizza stone or a cookie sheet (baking tray) lined with greased foil at the bottom of the oven and preheat to 425°F (220°C).

In a bowl toss blueberries with lemon juice, zest, sugar, cornstarch and salt. Mix well, but carefully, so as not to break the blueberries.

On a floured surface, roll out the other disc large enough for a 12-in (30cm) top crust. Take the pie dish from the fridge, place the blueberries into it, cover with the top crust, seal the edges with a fork moistened with water. Cut a criss-cross in the middle of the pie crust to allow air to escape.

Bake on top of the greased preheated stone or cookie sheet for 40–45 minutes until the blueberries bubble through the open slats. After 30 minutes, cover the edges of the pie with a foil ring to prevent burning.

Cool before serving.

Strawberry Preserves

Tangy wild strawberries in season are fantastic for preserves. Blueberries are also excellent. Since they're not as sweet, they require a little more sugar, one pound of sugar per one pound of blueberries. Blueberry jam is Tatiana's favorite, but she makes strawberry for her husband who is "sick to death of blueberries."

The foam that rises as the jam cooks is Alexander's favorite part of the preserves. He stands at the hearth, bent over the cast-iron pot, waiting for the jam to boil. At the critical point he pushes Tatiana aside so he can skim it himself.

Tatiana forges her way back to the pot, admonishing him for removing actual preserves along with the foam. He never listens.

Tatiana likes the preserves over bread in the morning, or at night with tea instead of sugar, in the Russian tradition. Alexander just likes the skim off the strawberries, any time of day or night.

Use 1¼ lb (570g) of sugar per 2lb (900g) of berries. Make
  sugar syrup first.

The Sugar Syrup:

1 cup (225ml) hot water
2¼ cups (570g) sugar

In a 3½-quart (3.15-liter) heavy-bottom saucepan, pour hot water over sugar until it melts, then bring to boil and simmer, stirring constantly for 2–3 minutes. Take off heat. Skim with a skimming ladle.

For the preserves:

Use 2 pounds of fresh strawberries, uniform and undamaged. Cut off the leaves and stems. Add strawberries to the hot sugar syrup, and leave for 3 hours. Then bring to a boil, and cook for 7 minutes, making sure the foam doesn't spill over the top of the pan. Skim as necessary. Turn off the heat and leave for 2 hours. Bring back to boil, and cook again for 7 minutes, skimming as necessary. Take off the heat and leave a further 2 hours. Finally, bring back to boil a third time, and cook for 20 minutes, skimming thoroughly, as necessary, until the strawberries are cooked through and translucent in color. Take off the heat, skim for the last time, cover with two layers of cheesecloth, and cool completely. Place in jars, seal, and, because you can, refrigerate.

The Famous, the One and Only Potato Pancakes

Tatiana was so young and silly when she made these for the first time—awkward, shy, with no confidence in her cooking abilities— because she had no cooking abilities. She had never heard of potato pancakes before, but Alexander suggested them, and she made them for him. Usually in the context of telling Tatiana why she was doomed to die an old maid, her Babushka Maya had been imparting the knowledge of generations of women, telling her that the way to a man's heart was through his stomach, and so Tatiana made Alexander potato pancakes to get into his heart.

He said they were great; even her family approved. They had them with homemade apple sauce and sour cream.

In Lazarevo, when Tatiana and Alexander got married, they had only a few things to cook. Blueberries. Cucumbers and fish. When Tatiana could get flour, she made pie with cabbage, onions and mushrooms. They ate pancakes, or black bread for breakfast. They had milk, they had tea. They had potatoes. And so she made him his favorite pancakes, and here's the recipe for them, though Tatiana maintains that if you're newly married and are making these for your smitten and grateful groom, there is no guarantee you will get to eat them hot.

But they taste good cold, too.

2½ cups (560g) raw potatoes, peeled, grated and squeezed
   dry of liquid
¼ cup (40g) grated onion
3 eggs, beaten
2 tablespoons all-purpose (plain) flour
1 teaspoon salt
¼ cup (55ml) canola oil
Optional:
sour cream
red caviar
apple sauce to taste

In medium bowl, combine potatoes, onion, eggs, flour, and salt. Heat oil in frying pan on medium-high heat. Drop potato mixture onto griddle and spread into 3-in (7.5 cm) pancakes. Reduce heat to medium. Cook until brown on bottom, flip with spatula, cook on the other side until crisp. Serve with sour cream and red caviar, or with some apple sauce. Alexander also liked his pancakes just plain with scrambled eggs on the side, or sunny-side-up eggs right on top.

Years later, in New York, and years later still in Arizona, Tatiana's friends, her children, her children's wives, and their children, and their teachers, and their children would ask her, "Where did you learn to cook like that?" And often she didn't know what to say. She wished she could say what other people say. Oh, my mother taught me, or, my grandmother taught me. But she just said, "Oh, I picked it up here and there." Or, if speaking to her children, said, "I learned to cook to please your father."

What she didn't say was this. I never would have known how to cook a single thing. Cooking was adult. And I was a child, and content to be a child until I *had* to grow up. I didn't want to because all the grown-ups I knew weren't happy, and I was happy. But there came a time in my life when there was no food to cook, no food to eat, and no food to buy. Nor were there lines anymore for anything, except for bread made of sawdust. Soup was just boiled water with salt. There was no flour for pies, no cabbage, no potatoes. There were no mushrooms and no apples. There was a blizzard outside our broken windows and not much else. During that time when we were without electricity, I lay in the dark next to my sister, with our mother and father dead, our grandparents dead, our brother gone, when it was just the two of us, and, to pass the minutes and hours while we were waiting for death or Alexander, whichever came first, I asked her to tell me how she made *blinchiki*, mushroom soup, apple pie, Napoleon, and Beef Stroganoff. And Dasha told me. We felt a little better talking about the food. She felt a little better talking about the food she would never have again. That's how I know how to cook.

CHAPTER THREE

Alone in New York
with Seven Million Others

On the White Star headed from Liverpool, England, to Ellis Island, Tatiana whispered lines of Pushkin to herself for perverse comfort. *"Eugene looks round—boat on a station!/He greets it like a revelation/ Calls to the ferryman—and he/ with daring unconcern is willing/ to take him for a quarter-shilling/across that formidable sea."* She whispered this like a mantra to herself until she got sick and weak and couldn't whisper anymore. Only her mouth moved, continuing to make the soundless words. *"Eugene looks round—boat on a station!/He greets it like a revelation/ Calls to the ferryman—and he/ with daring unconcern is willing/to take him for a quarter-shilling/across that formidable sea . . ."*

She was convinced that the rest of her life was going to be lived without Alexander. It took her a long time to lift her head, to raise her eyes, to agree to leave Ellis Island, to take a ferry across New York Bay to New York Island. It took her a long time, too, to get used to the idea of living. She didn't want to do it, but little by little, day by day, she put her feet forward, bought a carriage for her son, took him to New York. She did it for him. Ellis Island was no place for a little boy, living among the wounded and rejected, among the refugees; he didn't deserve it.

So, when her new friend, the beautiful and self-absorbed Vikki Sabatini, fellow nurse at the Ellis Island Hospital, invited her to the market on the Lower East Side, she went. And when Vikki invited Tatiana and Ant for Sunday dinner at her grandmother's, Tatiana went. She met Isabella. She tasted delicious food, and liked Vikki more because Vikki was so adored by her grandmother. When one Sunday Edward Ludlow, a doctor at the hospital, asked her to come play softball in Central Park, she took her boy, sat on the grass and watched a joyous American game. Edward offered her fresh strawberries. He had gone out to the farms and picked more than he could eat, so Tatiana ate them, and then made jam with the rest. The jam was good, and Edward was pleased, Vikki's grandparents, too, when Tatiana brought some for them. Vikki was pleased when she placed Anthony on her lap, the first time she had ever handled a child, and fed him a piece of soft white bread that he sucked on with his toothless gums, making a mess of her blouse but she didn't care.

This is how Tatiana, minute by minute and against her will, was pulled back into life.

Anthony kept growing, and his mother's milk was no longer enough. He loved food, and needed to be fed. He also needed to play with other kids, not stare at wounded soldiers. He needed life.

For Anthony's sake, Tatiana moved out of Ellis Island where she had eaten cafeteria food since his birth and found an apartment with Vikki. She started to cook again, things she remembered, things other than strawberry jam. She learned how to make Italian stuffed shells and Jewish challah rolls, chicken soup, and Chinese rice. She did as well as she could with her boy, a young widow living in New York. She tried to distance herself from the eager soldiers returning from war, yet not so far distant that she didn't peer into the faces of all the veterans to whom she brought her own *blinchiki*, her own *pirozhki*. Here, take this, she would say, take this, and tell me where he is. Tell me whether he's dead or alive, so I can walk as his widow or his wife.

No one would, or could, tell her, and so she continued to cook, and to learn new things all the while searching for an answer among the outcasts.

The way he carried his body, the way he walked in my life, Tatiana thought, declared that he was the only man I had ever loved, and he knew it.

And until I was alone without him, I thought it was all worth it.

Isabella's Pasta Sauce

Isabella, Vikki's grandmother, was from northern Italy unlike Alexander's mother who had been from Naples in the south, but one thing they both had in common was having made tomato sauce since before they could speak.

Tatiana had never tasted tomato sauce before she had dinner at Isabella's. Tomatoes grew poorly in Luga, were rarely grown, and were not often available in Leningrad. There was no olive oil, no basil, no parmesan cheese and all these tastes were unfamiliar to Tatiana. But after she went to Isabella's, she had second helpings and wondered if Alexander's mother had made something this delicious for him when they'd been living in Boston. How could she not have known this about him? How could he not have told her that once upon a time, he'd had this for dinner every Sunday? Sauce with meatballs and Italian bread.

½ cup (120ml) olive oil
2 tablespoons butter
1 medium or large onion, very finely chopped
10 large garlic cloves, finely chopped
58oz (1.65 kg) canned peeled tomatoes
16oz (450g) canned tomato sauce, or 2 cups (450ml)
  passata
3oz (75g) tomato paste
fresh basil leaves, uncut, or dried basil, 2 tablespoons
½ cup (50g) grated Parmesan cheese
½ cup (120ml) red cooking wine, or Marsala, or sherry
salt and pepper, to taste

Open the cans of tomatoes ahead of time. In a 9-quart (8.1-liter) heavy saucepan, heat the olive oil on medium-high. Melt the butter, then add the onions, cook 5–7 minutes until golden. If you're pressed for time, you can omit the onions and go to the next step—garlic.

Add garlic, cook in hot oil for no more than 30 seconds

(garlic burns like *that*), then immediately add the peeled whole tomatoes, tomato sauce, and tomato paste. Stir thoroughly, breaking up the tomatoes with a wooden spoon. If you don't like chunky sauce, use a hand-held mixer right in the pot to purée the tomatoes, onions and garlic to a creamy consistency. Add a cup of fresh basil leaves, stems removed. Isabella added a cup of grated parmesan directly into the sauce. Bring the sauce to boil, turn down the heat to the lowest setting, cover, and cook for as long as you can, preferably a few hours. Or you can cook for an hour, then take off the heat, and when cooled, refrigerate overnight. The sauce will taste even better the next day. Reheat slowly. Don't burn it, don't boil it, don't cover it completely.

Add the wine, Marsala or sherry half an hour before serving. Remove the fresh basil leaves.

Serve with meatballs and garlic bread—Italian bread sliced lengthwise, buttered and sprinkled with garlic powder and grated parmesan cheese—and a pinch of salt, then toasted in a 400°F (200°C) oven.

Isabella's Meatballs

2lb (900g) ground beef sirloin
1 small onion, grated
2 garlic cloves, grated
1 teaspoon dried basil or oregano
2 eggs

1 cup (50g) breadcrumbs, either homemade or store-bought.
    (To make fresh, take 4–5 slices of white bread and put
    through food processor. Makes beautiful breadcrumbs.)
salt and pepper, to taste
ice and ice water
olive oil or butter, for frying

Mix all together, then add two or so ice cubes. Stir until mixture is nice and cold. Leave the ice in the mixture while you make the meatballs. Make the meatballs from meat closest to the ice, small or big to your liking, and then either fry in a little olive oil or butter until they're nice and golden brown, or drop them straight into the sauce to cook. Either way the ice will make them nice and moist and the onion gives them a fantastic taste. Use fresh onion instead of onion powder. It tastes much better.

For sausage, use a pound of Italian sweet. Fry the sausages whole on medium heat until brown and crispy on all sides, drain lightly, drop into sauce. Don't poke holes in the sausage.

Parmesan Risotto

To everything Isabella made, she added parmesan cheese. "It's an Italian thing," she said. "Yes," agreed Tatiana. "The way Russians add sour cream." The way, later, her friend from Mexico added lime. The way Tatiana herself added onions. "It's a Tatiana thing," Alexander once said.

Vikki said, "Pass some more of that stuff with cheese."

"You cook, Vikki?" asked Tatiana.

"You know I don't," Vikki breezily replied. "Why ask?" Anthony was on her lap and she was feeding him tiny spoonfuls of rice with cheese.

Isabella shook her head. "It's hopeless, Tania. Don't even try. I've tried for years. She refuses to learn."

"I don't refuse to learn," said Vikki, doing her best to ignore them. "I choose not to. Right, Anthony? Right, little guy?"

"Well, someday," declared Isabella, "you're going to fall in love, and you'll learn how to cook so that he will love you."

"Indeed, Grammy. But how do you explain that I fall in love every five minutes and have not learned yet?"

"Is that what you call it, Viktoria Sabatini? Love?"

"Oooh, Grammy! Cutting. Biting."

"What do you think, Tania?" asked Isabella.

Tatiana wanted to be in on the joke. But she remained silent for a few moments. Then she spoke. "I think," said Tatiana, "that if he will not love her because she doesn't know how to make Parmesan risotto, he will not love her even if she learns to."

1 quart (900ml) chicken stock

1 tablespoon olive oil

1 small onion, very finely chopped

1 cup (200g) Arborio, or other Italian short-grain rice

2 garlic cloves, very finely chopped

3 tablespoons butter

⅓ cup (40g) grated Parmesan cheese

2 teaspoons salt, or to taste
black pepper, to taste
½ cup (50g) crumbled Gorgonzola cheese
Optional:
a few fresh, chopped sage leaves, or some fresh basil.

In a medium saucepan, bring chicken stock to boil, reduce heat. In a large heavy-bottom skillet, heat the olive oil on medium-high. Add onion, sauté for a few minutes, stirring. Add rice, stir to coat evenly. Add garlic, stir, continue to cook 30 seconds. Lower heat to medium and add half a cup of stock. Stir until liquid is absorbed but rice is not sticking to the bottom of the skillet. Continue adding stock, a little at a time, and stirring until all the liquid is absorbed, about 20 minutes.

Remove from heat, add butter, parmesan cheese, salt and pepper. Stir. Serve risotto in bowls or on plates, sprinkled with Gorgonzola cheese.

Mama's Chicken Soup

Mama used to make it. When Pasha got sick, it was all she made. It was so good, Tatiana used to wish Pasha would get sick more often; it was the only time she had the soup. "You're not sickly enough, Pasha," she used to say to him. "Unlike you, Tania," he would reply.

But in New York, the Jews on the Lower East Side made it, too, and it tasted just like Mama's. Tatiana liked that, the continuity of the recipe across the oceans. When Anthony got sick, that's what she cooked for him. When Vikki got sick, that's what she made for her. Although Vikki didn't get ill that often, she did get blue, breaking up with her beaus, looking for just *the* one, and when Vikki felt low, she wanted bread and soup. So, Tatiana made it for her friend and tried to teach her how to make it, too; it was so simple! When they no longer lived together, and Vikki had newly re-married, Tatiana asked if she made this soup for her husband, and her husband, Tom Richter, rolled his eyes and said, "I would die of a heart attack if my wife ever cooked me a single thing," and Vikki sheepishly said, "But, Tania, you know that it always tastes better when someone else cooks for you."

"Yes, like a wife," said Tom.

"Like Tania," rejoined Vikki.

"Tania can't be everybody's wife," stated Tom. "There are some wives that are just for one man," he added pointedly.

Next time Vikki and Tom came to spend a few days with her in Scottsdale, Tatiana made chicken soup for her friend who did not cook for her husband.

1 large, fat chicken with all the bones, the neck, and giblets.
  Throw the liver out.
10 cups (2.25 litres) water
1 large onion, peeled and left whole
2 bay leaves
1 small bunch parsley, tied with a piece of thread.
6 large carrots, peeled and sliced or cut into small chunks
3–4 stalks celery, leaves removed, sliced into ½-in (1 cm) pieces

1 medium parsnip, washed and peeled or not peeled. If you're
   planning to eat it, peel it. If you're planning to throw it out,
   leave the skin on for taste.
2 cups (330g) cooked white rice, to serve
salt, to taste

Wash chicken, place into large—at least 9-quart (8.1-
liter)—pot. Add water, onion, bay leaves, parsley, and salt,
and bring to boil. Turn down to a simmer, cover and cook
for 45 minutes. Add carrots, celery, and parsnip, bring back to
boil, cover again, and cook for another 45 minutes. Throw out
the onion, the parsley, and bay leaves. Adjust salt as necessary. Separate the chicken from the bone and shred. Leaving
the chicken on the bone is a very Russian thing to do.

Serve with the cooked rice. Don't add raw rice and cook in
the soup: it changes the taste of the broth—for the worse.

Chicken Curry

If America is the country of immigrants, then New York is the city
of immigrants, and they all cook. Tatiana, who greeted them at Ellis
Island, got the grain not the chaff of their cooking, and the people
she met living downtown were happy to share their lifeblood with
her, to share with her a little of what they'd carried with them into
the new land. And she, when she learned to cook from the Italians,
the Jews, the Russians, the Chinese, the Indians, carried a little bit
of their past into her bright, new, lonely life.

Prithvi from the Punjab taught her to make curry and, it was astonishing how Anthony devoured it, though the tastes were strong and unfamiliar. This recipe has quite a lot of liquid in it, so if your family doesn't like that you can reduce the two cans of chicken broth to just one. Tatiana's son loved the liquid, the more the better. He ate it with a spoon, like soup, but with more rice. And the next day, when there was no chicken left, he ate the rice with just the curry broth.

The curry Tatiana learned from a Punjabi man, the rice to go with it from a Cantonese. Chang Hao taught her about rice while recuperating from corneal scarring at Ellis Island. Tatiana couldn't pronounce his name. He told her to call him Tony. "Like your boy."

"My boy not Tony. He Anthony."

Chang Hao called for Anthony by waving his hand through the air and calling, "Tony, Tony, come here."

Anthony, eighteen months, on the floor playing with two trucks, never even looked up. Chang Hao tried to focus, then gave up. His highly contagious trachoma refused to get better, and he was facing certain deportation. Tatiana kept Anthony away but changed the man's eye dressings, gave him antibiotic faithfully every four hours and managed to save one eye. He was given a visa, opened a tiny place in Chinatown, and twice a week walked to Church Street to bring Tania and Anthony dinner. He brought her hot and sour soup and cold noodles with sesame sauce. He brought Anthony sesame chicken and shrimp Kung Pao. And he was the one who taught Tatiana how to make perfect white rice. "Americans, they overthink it," he said. "They wash, they rinse, they measure. They stir." He shook his head. "Rice is best left alone."

93

"You don't need to measure?" asked Tatiana, skeptically squinting as if optically damaged Chang Hao were her Babushka Maya.

"You don't need to measure," he confirmed. "You want perfect rice every time? Put your rice in the pan, pour cold water on it until water level reaches the first knuckle on your finger, about an inch above rice, add salt, add butter if you wish, I don't, but you can, then bring to boil on high heat. As soon as it boils, reduce heat to lowest low, cover, and forget about it for twenty minutes."

"And that's it?"

"That's it."

Chang Hao's business thrived in Chinatown for forty-five years and then was passed down to his grandchildren. And his way of making rice went just fine with chicken curry.

Chicken Curry:

3 tablespoons olive oil
3 tablespoon butter
5 garlic cloves, grated
5 tablespoons grated fresh ginger
1 large onion, very finely chopped or grated
2 tablespoons curry powder
1 tablespoon cumin
1 tablespoon garam masala
¼ teaspoon ground cardamom
2lb (900g) chicken breast fillets, cut into 1-in (2.5cm) pieces

1 tablespoon salt
1 Granny Smith apple
2 tablespoons all-purpose (plain) flour
4 cups (900ml) chicken stock
16oz (450g) canned tomato sauce, or 2 cups (450ml)
   passata
1 cup (225ml) half-and-half or yogurt

In a large, wide-bottom, heavy-bottom saucepan, heat 2 tablespoons oil and 2 tablespoons butter. Add garlic, cook briefly add ginger, cook for 1 minute. Add another tablespoon butter, add onion, cook until lightly golden. Add curry powder, cumin, garam masala and cardamom. Add the rest of the butter and olive oil, and the chicken. Cook on medium, turning occasionally until chicken starts to brown, 4–5 minutes. Add the salt and stir well. Peel and core apple, cut into quarters, add to the chicken. Add flour, stir to coat. Slowly add chicken stock and tomato sauce, stir well, cover and cook 30 minutes while you prepare the rice. After 30 minutes taste the curry and adjust the seasonings. You might need to add some more curry powder. Stir, cook for another minute or two, and take off the heat. Let stand for a minute or two and then add 1 cup of yogurt or half-and-half. Yogurt is delicious, but tends to separate inside the hot liquid, so stir constantly with a whisk until it's fully incorporated. Half-and-half goes in easily. Stir all to make creamy.

Serve with Chang Hao's basmati rice, p.94.

Macaroni and Cheese

Was Anthony suffering? Tatiana worked too much, and the hours were long. Isabella looked after the boy, but he was too often in the company of older people. Sometimes he went to the playground, but Tatiana feared it was not enough, couldn't be enough to make Anthony well. He was by nature too introspective, too solemn a little boy. She thought it was the food he ate. It wasn't American enough. He was always eating eggplant or peppers, or ossobucco. She wanted to learn to cook something fun for him, and perhaps in this way transform him into a fun American boy, his widowed Soviet mother notwithstanding.

When he went to nursery, her anxieties were realized. Anthony would come home and say the other kids were eating something called peanut butter and jelly. He had never had peanut butter and jelly. Butter made with peanuts? They had tunafish; what *was* that? They had snack items like pretzels; not Anthony.

Tatiana knew: working at Ellis Island, New York University and the Red Cross office was both too much and not enough. She needed to learn to do something else. What if Anthony's friends came over to play? She didn't want to be the kind of mother who served her son and his friends roasted peppers and rice for an afternoon snack.

So she bought peanut butter, and served him that on bread. She put some of her homemade strawberry jam on it. He liked it okay, but liked it even more when she cut an apple into cubes and let him dip the cubes into the peanut butter. She needed a tub of warm water to de-glue Anthony afterward, but he liked it, and this pleased her.

She began to experiment. She mixed apple cubes with cubes of muenster cheese. They were both white, and that was part of the fun—trying to figure out which was which before you touched a piece. She made Anthony tunafish with mayonnaise, a little lemon juice, salt, and instead of celery, which he didn't like, small slivers of apple. He loved it and asked for it every other day.

And because Tatiana believed there was no food that was not improved—to an incremental or revolutionary degree—by bacon, and because she assumed everyone else felt the same way, she served Anthony bacon. In the morning, she made him bacon and egg sandwiches. For lunch, grilled cheese and bacon sandwiches. She toasted bread, grilled the bacon to crisp and served it to him cut into quarters. For herself she added lettuce and tomato. For dinner she made macaroni and cheese—with bacon.

Tatiana had to grow into her macaroni and cheese recipe. It was too plain for her—and she couldn't imagine it as a meal in itself: where was the meat? So to make it more interesting, she tried different kinds of cheese, different spices, tried adding things to it, like bacon. Or ham. Or both. Finally, she devised a recipe that was so excellent, she started being asked to bring it to the nursery school for potluck afternoons and to Isabella's house on Sundays. Vikki requested it on a weekly basis. Mothers of her son's friends would call and ask how she made it, because little Billy was still talking about having it when he came to play. Tatiana started making American friends because of her macaroni and cheese.

Macaroni and Cheese:

1lb (450g) elbow macaroni, cooked
5 cups (1.125 liters) milk
1 large onion, peeled and left whole
5 tablespoons butter
5 tablespoons all-purpose (plain) flour
1lb (450g) extra sharp cheddar
8oz (225g) Swiss or Gruyère cheese
1lb (450g) mozzarella
1 teaspoon salt
pepper, to taste
½ teaspoon paprika
¼ teaspoon cayenne pepper
Optional:
bacon, cooked crisp, and chopped, or thick ham, small-cubed, and
  lightly fried

Preheat oven to 350°F (180°C). Butter a rectangular oven-proof casserole dish, 9×13 in (23×32.5cm).

In a medium saucepan heat milk and onion until bubbles just form around the edge of the pan. Turn off heat, and let onion infuse in the milk. Shred all the cheeses into separate bowls.

Meanwhile, melt butter in a 5-quart (4.5-liter) saucepan on medium heat. Add flour, and cook, stirring gently in a clockwork fashion 3–4 minutes. Discard the onion from the milk and slowly add milk to the roux paste, stirring constantly. Heat until milk mixture thickens and starts to bubble slightly. Add salt, pepper, paprika and cayenne. Remove from heat and add cooked macaroni. Add half the cheddar cheese, half the Swiss cheese, and half the mozzarella and mix thoroughly. Spread into the prepared ovenproof dish. Sprinkle with the rest of the cheddar, Swiss, and mozzarella cheeses. Bake for 30 minutes until cheese is bubbling.

Optional:
Crumb 8 strips of crisply-cooked bacon and fold it into the mac'n cheese before you sprinkle with cheeses and bake.

Cube 8oz (225g) thick ham, brown for a minute or two in a frying pan and add to the mac'n cheese.

Add both, bacon *and* ham. It's pretty unbelievable. Alternatively, serve the mac and cheese with ham on the side.

Chocolate-Chip Cookies

Anthony came home bringing the moist remains of a thoroughly chewed cookie and said, almost accusingly, "Rebecca's mother made these for Friday snack."

Tatiana looked, tasted. "What is it?" she asked suspiciously.

"A cookie, Mama."

"Hmm."

"A chocolate-chip cookie." It sounded even more accusing because it was said in Russian.

So Tatiana tried. But in Russia there had been no brown sugar, and so she didn't put any in, not knowing it wasn't a chocolate-chip cookie without the brown sugar.

"Mom, what is this?" Anthony said. "It's a sugar cookie with chocolate chips in it."

Tatiana tried again. She put in an extra cupful of chocolate chips. Anthony was critical. Vikki less so, but she said, "Tania, where's the brown sugar?"

"The what?"

"See, that's your problem right there. Buy some brown sugar, and you'll fix these right up."

Brown sugar? White sugar was what the aristocracy ate in Russia because it was refined and expensive, just right for their delicate palates. Centuries were spent in technocratic morass trying to work out a way to make brown sugar white. And now, suddenly, when she had the kingly white sugar in abundance, she needed brown sugar, in *America*?

Dutifully she went and bought brown sugar.

Anthony declared them too chewy.

"Anthony, you too picky," Tatiana said to him in English. "Just eat cookie and say thank you."

But the next evening, she made them crispy by adding a tiny bit of water to the mix. A finally approving Anthony wanted to bring some for snack the next day, but he and Vikki devoured them.

It was Rebecca's mother who called Tatiana and asked if Rebecca could come over. "Oh, and she's raving about the cookies your son brought to school the other day. You wouldn't happen to have the recipe, would you?"

"Oh, sure."

"And what about the little ones with the jam in them? She brought one home last week, it was excellent."

"Sure, you come, I give you cookies."

"May I have the recipe? I want to make them for my husband. He just came back from war and has a terrible sweet-tooth. You'd think they didn't feed him in the army."

Quietly Tatiana said, "Probably they not give him cookies with jam."

Chocolate-Chip Cookies:

2 cups (250g) all-purpose (plain) flour

1 teaspoon salt

1 teaspoon baking soda

2 sticks (225g) unsalted butter, softened

¾ cup (150g) dark-brown sugar

¾ cup (170g) white sugar

2 eggs

1 teaspoon vanilla extract

½–1 teaspoon water

1½ cups (250g) semi-sweet chocolate chips

Preheat oven to 350°F (180°C). Grease 2 cookie sheets (baking trays).

Gently stir together flour, salt, baking soda.

In the bowl of an electric mixer, cream together butter, white sugar, dark-brown sugar. Add eggs and vanilla and mix lightly. Add water, mix lightly. Carefully stir in the flour, followed by the chocolate chips. Don't overstir, or the cookies will harden.

Drop onto cookie sheets using a teaspoon and a tablespoon. For the little tots, dropped teaspoons will do. For the adults a tablespoon might be better. Make them as big or as little as you wish. Cookies will spread while cooking so give them plenty of room.

Bake for 10–12 minutes (less for smaller cookies) or until the edges have browned. Leave for 5 minutes on the cookie sheet, then transfer to a wire rack to cool.

Russian Tea Cookies

With jam. For Anthony. And for Rebecca's father who had recently returned from war and didn't get much dessert in the army.

Anthony only liked the jam. The cookie was just a receptacle for the fruit and sugar.

1 stick (110g) unsalted butter, softened
½ cup (100g) sugar
1 egg, separated
1 teaspoon vanilla extract
1 cup (125g) all-purpose (plain) flour
1 cup (110g) walnuts

raspberry jam
powdered (icing) sugar, for sprinkling

Preheat oven to 325°F (170°C). Grease cookie sheets.
In the bowl of an electric mixer cream butter and sugar.
Add egg yolk and vanilla and beat well. Carefully stir in flour,
either by hand or on lowest setting of the mixer.

Roll dough to the size of small meatballs. Process the walnuts in a food processor, or crush into fine crumbs in a mortar
and pestle. Spread out on a piece of waxed paper. Dip dough
balls in unbeaten egg white, then roll in the walnuts. Place
on cookie sheet and push the middle down with your thumb.
Bake for five minutes, then press the centers down again
with the back of a spoon. Bake for 15 minutes longer until
golden.

Fill the middle with half a teaspoon of raspberry jam. Plum
jam is good, too, as is cherry. The slightly sour jams work
better to contrast with the sweetness of the cookie than, say,
strawberry or apricot, though by all means, try the one you
like best.

When the cookies cool, sprinkle with powdered (icing)
sugar. They won't last the night. Anthony would eat the tray
of them. Actually, what he did was eat the jam out of the
centers and lick the sugar off every cookie, then nibble
around the edges, pretending to leave them behind. It was
like a little mouse had gotten to the Christmas pastry when
the family wasn't looking, thinking no one would notice.

"Anthony, you just like your mama," Tatiana said to him.

"I don't want to be like you, Mama," said Anthony. "I want to be like my dad."

The Best Hard-boiled Eggs

When Tatiana knew she was going to Germany to find Alexander and leaving her son behind with her best friend, one of the things she worried about was what Anthony was going to eat. Tatiana knew Vikki would love him, she knew she would take care of him, that he would be clean and dressed, that he might even make it to school on time, certainly more on time than Tatiana could make him, but the food concerned her. What would Ant and Vikki do every evening, every weekend?

"Vikki, be honest with me. Is there anything you know how to cook?"

"Tania, I'm insulted. I won't even dignify that with an answer."

"Tell me. Do you know how to boil an egg?"

"God!"

"Do you?"

"If you're so concerned, why don't you just stay here and cook for us instead of hopping off on a suicide mission?"

"Vikki, I repeat my question. I will repeat as many times as necessary. Do you know how to cook an egg?"

"I don't like eggs," Vikki said loftily.

"Well, Easter is coming soon."

"Easter? And *where* is this Easter coming? Are you joking with me? Easter is not for two months!"

"Like, I said. Soon. How are you going to color eggs—"

"Wait, wait." Vikki started to hyperventilate. "Are you telling me you're not planning to come back until *after* Easter?"

"Vikki, you ask me unknowable. How I know when I come back? If I find him in two weeks, I come back in two weeks."

"Yes, but . . ." Vikki almost didn't know how to ask. "What if you don't find him for two years?"

Now it was Tatiana's turn not to answer.

"And Tania . . ." Vikki had to sit down for her next question. "What if . . . what if . . . you don't find him at all?"

Tatiana sat down herself. Finally she answered. "Better let me teach you how to make eggs, Vikki."

"Anthony has never asked me to cook for him," Vikki said many years later. "What a blessing."

"Not just for you," said Anthony. "Besides, it's not true, Vik. Sometimes you cook. You make eggs." They were sitting in Tatiana's kitchen. It was the mid-seventies.

"Yes. But you never *asked* me to make eggs."

Alexander and Tatiana exchanged looks.

"What eggs? You mean hard-boiled eggs?" Tatiana asked slowly. "The kind Ant liked when he was little?"

"Mom, I never liked them."

"He still likes them," Vikki said defiantly.

Anthony rolled his eyes. "I hate them."

Alexander said, "Vikki, what have you done all these years when men expected you to cook for them?"

"I avoided men that did."

"Well, I suppose you had to narrow the field somehow."

"Tania, reign in your husband," returned Vikki without pause, as if they were in an ad-lib comedy troupe. "Besides, I know how to cook. I told you, I can make eggs."

"Do eggs even count as a recipe?"

"Ask Ant. He loves eggs."

"I hate eggs."

Vikki continued undaunted. "Besides, you said so yourself—it's a blessing I don't come anywhere near a stove."

Anthony deflected diplomatically. "Your hard-boiled eggs *are* pretty good. After all, you've gotten a lot of practice. It's the only thing you know how to make."

"It was the only thing your mother taught me!"

"Don't lie, Vikki," said Tatiana. "It was the only thing you remembered how to do."

"For your information, you smart-ass Barringtons," said Vikki, "because I can see you've forgotten a few things yourselves—the only reason I had to learn how to cook at all is because someone, I won't mention any names, galloped off to Germany to find someone, I won't mention any names and left me with—"

"Vikki!" That was Tatiana, Anthony, and Alexander. She laughed. They fell quiet.

Unapologetic, ignoring Anthony's glaring eye, Vikki said, "Last time we'll be talking about my lack of cooking abilities, then? That's too bad. Because I was just beginning to enjoy this conversation."

eggs
water
salt

Place eggs in cold water that covers them just to the top.
Add salt to keep the eggs from cracking, a heaping tablespoon or two. Bring to boil. As soon as water boils, turn off
the heat, cover completely, and let stand for 10 minutes.
Drain, cool, eat, color, use in recipes.

To color eggs, use food coloring, a dozen drops mixed with
three tablespoons of white vinegar and half a cup of cold
water. Use more drops for more intense color, and place the
eggs right into the cup. The longer the eggs are left, the
darker their color will be. Take them out and let them dry.

Paskha

Tatiana was in Germany, and Anthony and Vikki were alone in
the apartment. He had been such a verbal boy, but after his mother
left, he behaved as if he'd lost his ability to speak. He played with
his friends, on the swings, in playgroup. He played hide-and-seek
with Vikki. She read to him. He let her hold his hand when she
took him to her grandmother's, when she took him to nursery
school. He walked to her when she came to pick him up. When she
asked what he wanted for dinner, he, almost as if knowing that
Vikki would have trouble cooking, said, "I don't care."

"How about bacon?"

"Just bacon?"

"Bacon on bread?"

"OK."

Often they ate out. Chang Hao still brought his Chinese food twice a week. Isabella cooked one weekly meal, plus her dinner on Sundays. Saturdays they went out for pizza. The rest of the time they had bacon sandwiches.

With Easter coming up, Vikki managed to boil the eggs the way Tatiana taught her, to color them. And then Anthony said, "What about Paskha?" Paskha was the traditional cheesecake-like Russian dessert prepared to celebrate Easter.

"What about it?"

"Aren't we going to make Paskha?"

"Anthony . . ."

"Mama told you how. I heard her." That was more than he had spoken in weeks. Encouraged, Vikki said, "Of course we'll make Paskha. To celebrate the Feast of Feasts, why not? It just doesn't say Easter if we don't have cheese dripping water onto our floor. But you'll help me, right? I'm going to need your help, Ant."

"That's what Mama said."

"She said that, did she?"

Paskha:

3lb (1.35kg) farmer cheese or ricotta
4 sticks (450g) unsalted butter, softened

2½ cups (560g) sugar
8 egg yolks
1 cup (225ml) heavy whipping cream
2 teaspoons vanilla extract
1 teaspoon ground cardamom
Optional:
1 cup (175g) golden raisins or sultanas

Run farmer cheese through the ricer twice into a large mixing bowl to make it as smooth as possible.

In the large bowl of a stand mixer cream butter with 1 cup (200g) sugar until the mixture becomes like thick sour cream.

Fold into farmer cheese until smooth.

Cream the egg yolks with 1 cup (200g) sugar until white. Fold into the cheese mixture.

Whip the heavy cream with the remaining ½ cup (100g) sugar until it becomes soft and thick.

Fold carefully into the cheese mixture.

Add vanilla and cardamom, and golden raisins or sultanas if using.

Fold the mixture into a cheese cloth, folded over two or three times, and hang like a hanging plant over a pot to catch the liquid for 12–24 hours. After it's set, refrigerate. Or, you can rig something up in the fridge, as long as it's hanging a few inches off the bottom shelf. Using a prepared Paskha mold doesn't drain it properly and leaves it too soggy. It's good to get as much moisture out as possible.

Anthony and Vikki sat at the table. Easter had come and long gone, it was miserably wet and cold outside, and they hadn't been to the playground for a week. This Saturday they remained in the apartment, cleaning, reading, playing hide-and-seek. Now it was dinner time. She was glaring at him, he stared back, unfazed. He would soon be three. She tried humoring him. But Anthony would be humored only when he felt like being humored. The dinner remained untouched on his plate.

"Come on, bud, you got to eat something. Eat a little."

"Don't want to. We had it five hundred times and forty-six. We had it for eighty-seven minutes in a row. Don't want to."

"Anthony, we've had it twice!"

"All the time. I want cabbage pie."

"I don't know how to make cabbage pie."

"I want fresh bread."

"I don't know how to make that."

"I want mushroom soup."

"I can't make it."

"I want cookies with jelly in the middle."

"Can't make those. I'll give you some jelly, though. It's the only thing you eat anyway."

"Didn't my mama tell you how to make them?"

"She told me how to make eggs. She told me how to make tuna."

"I don't want tuna!"

"Well, it's on your plate, Anthony, and there's nothing else. So eat it."

"Don't want to."

"You're not doing anything else until you finish it."

"Fine."

They sat for a few minutes longer.

"Ant," said a defeated Vikki, "want to go to Grammy's? I'm sure there'll be pasta."

"Don't want pasta."

"So what do you want?" Vikki snapped. And looked away. Anthony was quiet. They didn't speak while the water dripped from the faucet, while the rain dripped outside. "Ant," Vikki said, brightening, "want to go up to Aunt Esther's?"

"Yes," the boy said instantly. "Yes! Rosa makes bread pudding. I love bread pudding. And the meat thing. Meat in a pot. I like that."

Aunt Esther was Alexander's father's sister. She lived near Boston with her housekeeper Rosa, who had taken care of Alexander when he had been a small boy himself.

When they were walking in the rain under an umbrella to take the bus to Grand Central Station to spend a week with Aunt Esther, Vikki, holding Anthony's hand, said, "I'm doing the best I can, bud. It's not easy, you know."

"I know. When is Mama coming home?"

"Soon, bud. Real soon."

CHAPTER FOUR

Aunt Esther

Vikki and Anthony were on the train heading up to Barrington where Esther lived. They were both next to the window. Anthony was making palm prints on the glass. Vikki stared out at the passing scenery. Now Anthony was the one who had cheered up, and Vikki was gloomy.

"You gloomy like a Sunday," said Anthony, quoting a popular song that was being played on the radio. Vikki grumbled something to him about things he wouldn't understand, about being invited to go dancing by no less than three perfectly good naval gentlemen recuperating from the war. "Why so gloomy?" Anthony pressed on. "Hungry? You will have food soon. You will have pot meat and maybe a punkin pie."

"No, Ant," said Vikki, squeezing and tickling Anthony sitting on her lap, now squirming. "No pumpkin pie in spring. Pumpkin pie in the fall. And we have food at home, too."

"We have no food. We have eggs. I want bread pudding."

In Barrington, Esther and Rosa were elated to see Anthony. Esther, as usual, begged Vikki to leave him with them, "Just to give you a little break, sweetheart. You're so young and pretty. Don't you want to go dancing?"

"Me?" said Vikki, with a casual wave of the hand. "Oh no, not me. I don't dance, no. I'm just here, looking after Ant until Tania comes back."

"Give yourself a little break, honey," said Rosa.

"No, no break necessary. I'm fine. Really," she added, seeing their skeptical faces, seeing Anthony's skeptical face. "I'm fine. I have nothing to do. Just look after the boy. Besides, I promised Tania."

Esther and Rosa spent the week playing with Anthony and cooking. Vikki slept till noon, stayed up late, ate the food they made, had her clothes washed and ironed. The weather cleared, warmed up; it got sunny. They went down to the beach, flew kites, collected sea shells, took pictures. They had a picnic in the chilly April wind on Nantucket Sound, waded in the icy water in their bare sandy feet. Anthony ran after the squawking sea gulls like a little boy, finally.

And morning, noon, and night, he was fed like a king. Food was brought to him, and fed to him. He was asked what he wanted, and no request was denied. So when Anthony said he wanted meat in a pot, he got pot roast. When he said he wanted corn soup, he got winter chowder. When he said "punkin pie," there was Rosa, making Anthony a punkin pie in the spring.

And Vikki, who had been fed like this all her life by the grandmother who raised her, watched it all and understood.

Pot Roast

Start with the most expensive cut of meat you can afford. There is no escaping it—the more expensive the meat, the better the pot roast. Rump roast is good, bottom round. Top round. Shoulder roast. Beef grills and roasts better in peanut oil than olive oil.

4–5lb (1.8–2.25kg) rump roast
5 tablespoons peanut or canola oil
1 large onion, coarsely sliced
4 garlic cloves, coarsely sliced
6 large potatoes, peeled and quartered, or 10–12 small new
    potatoes, peeled and left whole
6 carrots, peeled and cut into 2-in (5cm) chunks
1 11oz can Campbell's Tomato Bisque soup, or any other can
    of concentrated tomato soup, or an 8oz (225g) can plain
    tomato sauce, or 1 cup (225ml) passata
1 cup (225ml) beef broth or water
1 cup (225ml) red cooking wine
salt and pepper, to taste

Leave rump roast out of the fridge for 30 minutes, then rub with salt and pepper. Heat oil in large heavy-bottom pot. Brown meat on all sides, until rich dark brown, about 4 minutes a side. While meat is cooking, throw the onions all around the meat, and brown them, too. Add garlic. Add potatoes, carrots, tomato soup, broth or water, wine, cover completely and cook in oven at 275°F (140°C) for 5 hours, or 325°F (170°C) for 4 hours, or 350°F (180°C) for 3 hours, checking to make sure there is enough liquid. If you keep the lid tightly closed, you shouldn't have a problem. Serve with warm bread.

Macaroni and Beef Casserole

Esther told Vikki she had taught Alexander's mother how to make this, and Jane Barrington made it for Harold and Alexander when they still lived in the United States. Alexander liked it, but Harold had loved it, and Alexander grew to like it more because his father liked it. And now, when Aunt Esther made the casserole for Anthony, who liked it okay, she said to him, "This was your daddy's favorite meal when he was a little boy," and Anthony liked it more because his father had liked it.

2 tablespoons butter
1 onion, very finely chopped
3 garlic cloves, grated
1½lb (700g) ground beef sirloin
1lb (450g) elbow macaroni, partially cooked and drained
1 cup (50g) fresh breadcrumbs
4 tablespoons melted butter

You can make simple sauce for this recipe, or you can use some leftover sauce, if you have any.

To make simple sauce:

¼ cup (55ml) olive oil
2 tablespoons butter
6 garlic cloves, grated
48oz (1.35 liters) plain canned tomato sauce, or passata
salt and pepper

Preheat heavy-bottom pot on medium-high, about 2 minutes, add oil, heat another 2 minutes, turn down to medium. Add garlic and sauté 30 seconds. Add tomato sauce and adjust seasoning. Bring to boil, turn down heat and simmer, covered, while you prepare the other ingredients.

In a heavy skillet, heat the butter, fry onion until slightly golden, add garlic, cook 30 seconds, add meat, brown, add salt, pepper to taste.

Cook the pasta al dente, drain, and add a little butter. Add the beef mixture and tomato sauce, stir well. Turn out into a prepared, greased large casserole dish. Sprinkle with 1 cup (50g) breadcrumbs and 4 tablespoons melted butter. Bake at 350°F (180°C) until breadcrumbs are crunchy and golden. Serves 150. Just kidding. Makes great leftovers.

Winter Chowder (in Spring)

3 leeks
8 slices bacon, cut into ½-in (1 cm) pieces
3 large all-purpose potatoes
1 large head celery
1 butternut squash or 2 zucchini
2 cups (450 ml) chicken broth
2 cups (450ml) water
½ teaspoon dried thyme
1 teaspoon salt, or to taste
½ teaspoon black pepper
1 cup (225ml) half-and-half, or equal quantities of cream and
  milk

Rinse leeks very well in cold water, make sure to get out all the sand and grit, then cut off roots and dark leafy tops. Cut each white stalk lengthwise, then crosswise into ½-in (1 cm) pieces. Rinse again, if necessary.

Preheat a large heavy-bottom skillet on medium. Fry the bacon pieces until they're wilting and the fat is released. Add leeks, cook together with the bacon, stirring occasionally, until both brown, about 10 minutes. Meanwhile, peel the potatoes and cut into small chunks. Wash celery, cut into ½-in (1 cm) chunks. Cut squash or zucchini open, discard seeds. Peel and cut into 1-in (2.5 cm) chunks.

Place potatoes, celery, squash (or zucchini), chicken broth, water, thyme, salt and pepper into a 6-quart (5.4-liter) pot, add leeks and bacon. Mix well, bring to boil, turn down the heat to the lowest simmer, cover completely, and simmer for 90 minutes until all vegetables are soft.

Remove 2 cups of the vegetables, mash them with a fork, return to broth, add half-and-half, stir, heat through, and serve.

To vary:
omit celery, add ½ cup (75g) frozen corn, or ½ cup (75g) frozen mixed vegetables, or 1 cup (150g) thinly sliced raw carrots.

Ham à la Cordone

Cathy Cordone was Esther's next-door neighbor in Barrington. Every New Year's Eve, she would come with her husband and son to Esther and Rosa's and bring not a Napoleon, but a ham with brown sugar glaze. The war put a stop to large hocks of ham, but at the end of 1945, right before Tatiana went to Germany, she came to spend New Year's Eve with Esther and Rosa, bringing Vikki and Anthony, and got a taste of Cathy's ham, newly bought, and glazed. As she was eating, and only half-listening to Esther telling her how much Alexander had once liked ham, (was there anything Alexander did not like?) and how much Harold liked ham (was there anything Harold had not liked?) and how Esther bet there had been no ham in the Soviet Union ("You are right about that, Esther, there wasn't much."), Tatiana's mind wondered. She recalled how she had journeyed to Iowa, and had spoken to the mother of the soldier who had been approached in the remote castle of Colditz by a man named Alexander Barrington; how she had been in touch with Sam Gulotta, her contact in the State Department, and had heard the curator of the Hermitage Museum, Josif Orbeli, explode his name into her heart and testify to the reasons he got his most precious works of art out of a besieged city.

And so, as Tatiana ate Cathy Cordone's New Year's Eve feast, she knew that Alexander was not dead but alive, knew she was not a widow but a wife, and thought how much Alexander would have enjoyed a piece of ham, and wondered, too, how long it had been since he had likely had one.

The Marinade: (Prepare two days before your event.)

4 garlic cloves, grated
4 teaspoons grated fresh ginger
1 cup (220ml) sweetened pineapple juice
½ cup (110ml) maple syrup
¼ cup (55ml) soy sauce
Place in medium bowl, mix, refrigerate overnight.

The Ham:

A whole ham
25–30 cloves
1 can sliced pineapple with juice

One day before your event, buy the ham: uncut, unspiraled, unbasted, as plain as can be, still on the bone. Score the ham in a diamond pattern and set with cloves in the crosscuts. You'll need about 25–30 cloves for a whole ham. Then pour the prepared marinade over the ham, making sure it gets inside all the diamond cuts. Cover and refrigerate overnight.

The day of the event, preheat the oven to 350°F (180°C), baste with the marinade, cover loosely with foil, place in oven, and heat 1 hour, basting every 15 minutes. After an hour, take off the foil and heat uncovered another hour, basting every 15 minutes. Half an hour before it's done, put the pineapple slices on top. Pour a little pineapple juice over.

Great potluck party dish—but also, if you're hiding your family on an island no one ever heard of called Bethel, living on the quay of one of the tributaries of Suisun Bay, hiding but pretending you're living, and it's Christmas, and your two men, your son and your husband, who at any moment can and will be wrenched away from you, are trying to catch a prehistoric sturgeon, this is a good dish to make for them to celebrate your brief yet eternal togetherness.

Rosa's Bread Pudding

"When Alexander was a little boy, I used to make this for him," Rosa told Anthony.

"I *know*. Did he love it?"

"He loved it like you."

"I love it a lot."

"Yes."

"Did he eat with large spoon right out of oven?"

"Yes. Like you."

"Did he burn his tongue?"

"Yes, dear boy. Just like you. Now be careful. It's awfully hot. Wait just a minute, just one minute, Anthony. I know it's good, but it's too hot—Anthony!"

Anthony began to cry because he'd burned his tongue.

"What did I tell you? You're impossible. Vikki!"

1 stick (110g) butter, plus 2 tablespoons, plus extra for greasing

1 quart (900ml–1liter) half-and-half or light cream, or 1 quart (900ml) milk

4 eggs, well beaten

½ cup (110g) sugar

½ cup (100g) brown sugar, plus 2 tablespoons for sprinkling

1 tablespoon ground cinnamon

1 tablespoon vanilla extract

10 slices white bread (You can use oatmeal bread, challah bread, buttermilk bread. Stay away from crusty loaves: they have too much water content and make for watery bread pudding.)

Preheat oven to 350°F (180°C). Butter a medium, deep ovenproof dish. In a heavy-bottom 3-quart (2.7-liter) saucepan, combine half-and-half, beaten eggs, sugars, cinnamon and vanilla, and bring to boil, then take off the heat. Wait five minutes, then add the stick of butter, and stir until it dissolves. Cut the crusts off the bread, reserve. In the prepared dish, arrange the white square pieces of bread in a single layer, pour some of the cream mixture over it. Arrange another layer, pour on more mixture. Continue layering until all the bread is gone. Crumble the crusts to make 1 cup (55g) crumbs, melt 2 tablespoons butter, mix with the breadcrumbs, sprinkle on top of the bread pudding. Sprinkle the 2 tablespoons brown sugar on top of the breadcrumbs. Bake for 45 minutes in the preheated oven. Cool slightly, eat while still warm. Serve with whipped or heavy cream. Refrigerate the rest. It's good cold, too.

After they came back home, Vikki tried to make bread pudding for Anthony, but she put in too much bread and not nearly enough milk. There was stuff in that recipe that didn't make sense to Vikki. Why would the bread suddenly expand so much as to overflow the pot? Why did the butter burn on the bottom? Why wasn't it sweet enough? Did she put in too much cinnamon or too little? Nothing made sense. Yet the boy ate it pretty happily every time, and asked for more.

And then one day in July, she picked up Anthony from playgroup, and took him to Battery Park. After he'd played on the swings,

Vikki bought him ice cream, and they sat on a bench looking at New York Harbor.

Vikki said, "Ant, I have to tell you something."

"What?"

"I have good news."

"You made bread pudding?"

"Even better."

"Better than bread pudding?"

"Hard to believe, but yes. Your mama is coming home."

Anthony jumped up, his ice cream dripped. Then he sat back down. He sat next to Vikki and didn't say anything. It was as if he were waiting. She waited, too. She waited for him to ask her, but when minutes went by and he didn't ask, she said, "In two weeks or so."

Still he didn't ask.

"She's bringing your dad home, too, Ant. Your daddy's coming home."

Anthony didn't say anything for a long while. He finished his ice cream, and they got up, and started walking home. Then Anthony spoke. Reaching up and taking Vikki's hand, he said, "Better make some bread pudding for him, Vikki."

CHAPTER FIVE

Deer Isle

Tatiana wished they could have days when they would never leave their tiny room. Because usually Alexander left early in the morning and didn't come back until he was worn-out and filthy after pulling up lobster traps for twelve hours.

But some evenings he read the paper to her and they went to sit on the bench by the bay to watch the sea gulls squabble for their own dinner. There were nights he was ravenous and days he was thirsty, and there were some nights when he lay turned away and could not bring himself to turn to her, when she kissed his bare back and wiped her own salty tears off his shoulders and whispered to his disconsolate soul, trying to soothe him, to soothe herself and failing that, lay behind him and cried.

"It's all a dream," he would whisper on those black nights. "It will all be gone, in a breath. Watch and see. All this, all this want and hope, washed into the Atlantic. Just watch."

"I can't tell, Alexander, are we happy?" she asked, her crying breath melting into his back. "Is this what we are? Delirious from joy?"

"Yes, this is the slow falling away into the land of enchantment."
She fell into silence.

"*Ya lyublyu tebya*, Tania."

"*Jäg älskar dig*, Shura."

Tatiana didn't cook much worth remembering in Deer Isle, except for lobsters, and breakfast for him. He was so distressingly underweight, so gaunt in his face and body that she tried to make him a breakfast before he went out on the boat, a breakfast big enough and filling enough to tide him over till lunch. She got up at four in the morning to make him toasted muffins with bacon or ham, fried egg and melted cheese, and something she called a soldier's breakfast, which Alexander seemed to actually like because he sometimes asked for it, even when it wasn't breakfast.

Tania's Soldier's Breakfast

4 large, all-purpose potatoes, about 1lb (450g)
½ cup (120ml) canola oil
2 tablespoons butter
4 eggs
1 long, thick stick of Italian bread
butter
salt and pepper, to taste

Peel the potatoes and dice them into small cubes. In a heavy-bottom pan heat ½ cup (120ml) canola oil and 2 tablespoons butter. When oil is very hot, add the potatoes, and cook on medium-high, stirring often, uncovered, for 15 minutes, until brown and crispy. Salt and pepper generously. When the potatoes are done, break four eggs over the top, salt them slightly, and cover to cook quickly, about 2 minutes.

Meanwhile, scoop out the inside of the crusty bread and toast lightly. Spoon the potato/egg mixture into the bread cavity. Eat. Breakfast of soldiers. Tatiana's soldier, back from the dead, went on the lobster boat in his tall rubber boots and his orange coveralls and didn't need anything else till the sun was at full noon.

CHAPTER SIX

Aunt Esther's Thanksgiving

Little by little things got better. After they left Deer Isle, the three of them drove down to Esther's where, as always, Esther made a feast, never forgetting to tell Tatiana that back when Alexander lived in Massachusetts with his family, this is what they would have every Thanksgiving. "Isn't that right, Alexander, darling?"

"Yes, Aunt Esther."

"We used to have such great Thanksgivings, didn't we?"

"Yes, Aunt Esther."

"Well, except that once when your father was in jail, and we couldn't bail him out in time. But otherwise very good, no?"

"Yes, otherwise very good."

And Aunt Esther would cry: "Your poor dad, Alexander."

"Yes. My mother, too."

"Of course, of course." But somehow Esther stiffened, as if secretly blaming Jane Barrington for the turn of events that took away her only brother and his only son and brought them to the Soviet Union, as if blaming her instead of blaming him for setting off a chain of events that led to their deaths because, in Esther's eyes, no matter how culpable he was, Harold would remain eternally blameless.

Tatiana kept careful watch, and helped Esther with dinner. She made the plum glaze for the turkey, cut the leeks for the stuffing, mashed the potatoes, made the gravy and the glaze for the sweet potatoes, and assembled the pumpkin pie. She added her own touch to the sweet potatoes, putting in a little orange juice and marshmallows on top—"For Anthony," she said, and Alexander said, "Not just for Ant. I love marshmallows."

"Tania, these sweet potatoes *are* exquisite," said Esther. "Did you put orange juice in them? Nice. Where did you learn how to cook?"

Ah, the infernal question. "New York has many fine cooks," replied Tatiana.

"Alexander, you are going to be one well-fed husband. You'll never be hungry."

Both Tania and Alexander looked down into their plates, filled with food, and forced their minds away from the things they could not forget. "That's true, Aunt Esther," said Alexander. "Once I was hungry, but Tania fed me."

"Well, then, I don't understand why you're still so thin. Tania, maybe you're not feeding him enough."

"Esther, the man never stops eating."

The man gave her a sideways glance.

"Why is he so thin then? Give him more, Tania. Give him more."

"Yes, Tania, I want some more."

128

And Tatiana cried.

Aunt Esther, now perfectly composed, said, "No, this girl—the waterworks are permanently turned on."

Roast Turkey

Later and on her own, Tatiana learned the hard way—defrost the turkey *completely* before cooking. This was the part of cooking the turkey that she kept forgetting, and once the fateful day arrived, it was too late. Leaving the turkey in the refrigerator was not enough—the turkey is an igloo, insulating the ice inside. On the day of the feast, she discovered that the turkey was perfectly soft on the outside while the inside remained solid. And when she cooked it, the outside became crisp—too crisp—then burnt, and the inside was red, pink, inedible. Turkey wasn't beef tenderloin. She couldn't leave a nice red center for the guests that liked their fowl rare. Since then she made sure it was defrosted through and through. On cooking day, she took it out of the fridge ninety minutes ahead of putting it in the oven. She guaranteed herself a moist, beautifully cooked turkey with a great red-golden glaze.

> 1 turkey, about 16–20lb (7.2–9kg), giblets removed
> small onion, or 1 leek, or a handful of shallots, roughly chopped
> 1 tablespoon whole peppercorns
> 2 carrots, roughly chopped
> about 6–7 tablespoons butter
> 1 teaspoon dried thyme

For the glaze:

4 tablespoons butter
½ teaspoon dried thyme
2 tablespoons water
salt and pepper, to taste
5oz (150g) dark jam, plum, cherry, raspberry

For the gravy:

6 tablespoons butter
6 tablespoons flour

Preheat oven to 415°F (210°C).

Take out giblets, wash turkey, pat dry. Don't throw giblets out, except for the liver. Place them in a medium saucepan with 2 cups of water, bring to the boil, turn down heat and simmer for an hour. You'll use the broth for gravy. Inside the empty cavity of the turkey place roughly cut up onion, carrots, peppercorns, salt and thyme. Tatiana also places a few dabs of butter inside and two ice cubes.

In a small bowl combine ¼ cup (50g) melted butter, add salt, mix well, brush all over the turkey.

Place the turkey on a rack inside a roasting pan and roast for 30 minutes. Meanwhile make the glaze. In a small pan, combine ¼ cup (50g) butter, salt, thyme, peppercorns, water, and 5 oz (150g) of jam. Bring to boil, reduce heat, and stirring occasionally cook for 10 minutes. Strain glaze through a sieve into a small bowl.

After 30 minutes, reduce heat for the turkey to 325°F (170°C), and baste with the plum glaze. Continue to cook, basting every 30 minutes or so, until the turkey thermometer pops out, or until the instant-read thermometer inserted into thickest part of breast, but not touching the bone, reads 165°F (74°C). Turkey will continue to cook after being taken out while it composes on your holiday table. Reserve the juices at bottom of pan for gravy. Leave the turkey out for 20–25 minutes while you prepare your gravy and vegetables. It looks beautiful on your table, but if you wish, you can cover it with aluminum foil to keep it from getting too cold.

Carve and serve with mashed potatoes (p.132), leek and bacon stuffing (p.133), cranberry jelly, string beans and gravy.

Gravy:

Remember the giblets you were cooking? Well, now you have delicious stock for gravy. Strain it through a mesh sieve, then add to the juices at the bottom of the roasting pan, and mix well until all the brown bits are absorbed into the broth. Strain again through a sieve, so that you're left with just dark, thick, smooth liquid.

In a heavy-bottom medium pan, melt 5 tablespoons butter on medium heat. Add 5 tablespoons all-purpose (plain) flour, and stir nonstop for 3–4 minutes. Slowly add the turkey stock to the roux, turn up the heat a little, and continue mixing until well-thickened and bubbles form at the sides. Don't boil. Makes about 5 cups.

Esther's Mashed Potatoes

The secret to these mashed potatoes is using half-and-half or light cream instead of milk. Tania's guests asked for seconds and thirds, finally admitting that they were the best mashed potatoes they'd ever had. There were some other things Tatiana did to flavor the potatoes. She served them on all holidays, with her Russian meat cutlets, and with turkey. She served them with beef tenderloin, and on top of shepherd's pie.

5lb (2.25kg) all-purpose potatoes, peeled and quartered
1 medium onion, peeled and left whole
2 garlic cloves, peeled and left whole
1 bay leaf
2 carrots, peeled or unpeeled
1 pint (600ml) half-and-half or light cream
1¼ sticks (150g) butter, melted
salt and pepper, to taste

Place potatoes along with onion, garlic, bay leaf and carrots into large pot and fill with water till just covered. Add salt.

Bring to boil, cover, reduce heat to medium or medium-low and simmer until potatoes are soft but not mushy, about 25 minutes. Drain and leave in colander. Discard the onion, garlic, bay leaf, carrots.

Meanwhile, heat the cream and melt butter. Put the potatoes through a ricer, into a serving bowl. With a ricer, unlike an electric beater, Tatiana got perfect, lump free mashed potatoes that were never like glue. After ricing the potatoes, add the cream and mix well with a wooden spoon. Add the melted butter and mix again. Adjust seasoning.

Bacon and Leek Stuffing

This replaced all other stuffing at Esther's table, it replaced all other stuffing at Tatiana's table, and it will replace all other stuffing at yours, too. Oh, you'll be tempted to get store-bought or to make your own with sausage and cornbread (also good). But soon it will become plainly apparent by the reaction of your guests that there's something about the combination of leeks and bacon with the thyme and turkey, the crunchiness of the stuffing, the aroma and the taste, that makes all other stuffings obsolete. This is the one thing Tatiana was always asked to bring when she asked if she could bring something. This and the Macaroni and Cheese with ham and bacon.

1 oval country white loaf
4 tablespoons butter
4–5 long thick leeks
2 garlic cloves, very finely chopped
4–5 medium carrots, thinly sliced

salt and pepper, to taste
thyme
10 slices bacon, cooked crisp and crumbled
1¼ cups (275ml) chicken stock
1 cup (225ml) milk

Cut the bread into cubes about 1-in (2.5 cm) thick and bake on a cookie sheet (baking tray) at 375°F (190°C) until golden and crispy, about 20 minutes. Empty into a large mixing bowl.

Meanwhile, wash leeks thoroughly, cut off the green part, leaving only the white, slice lengthwise to split the stalk in two, then cut into ½-in (1 cm) pieces.

Melt butter in a large, heavy-bottom frying pan. Add leeks, cook on medium about 7 minutes, stirring occasionally. Add garlic, carrots, salt, pepper, thyme and cook 5–7 minutes more. Add cooked, crumbled bacon, stir, take off the heat.

Add the leek mixture to the bread, add chicken stock and milk, and mix well. Turn out into a well greased rectangular 13×9in (32.5×23 cm) pan. Bake in a 350°F (180°C) oven about 45 minutes until crispy and crunchy on top.

Sweet Potatoes

There was no Thanksgiving for Tatiana without sweet potatoes. This recipe came from her friend Phil, an orderly at Ellis, who went to Montreal, Canada, for his master's, came back with no master's but with this recipe, and after trying it Tatiana declared that Montreal was worth it. The rum, orange juice and marshmallows are extra. Tatiana could do without the marshmallows, but not the rum. But Alexander and Anthony couldn't do without the marshmallows. You can always make two batches, one traditionally Canadian, and one like dessert.

Traditional:

4 large sweet potatoes
5 tablespoons butter
5 tablespoons dark maple syrup
5 tablespoons light brown sugar
Optional:
¼ cup (55ml) orange juice
¼ cup (55ml) dark rum
1 cup (50g) mini marshmallows

Peel the sweet potatoes. You might want to quarter them before cooking. Place potatoes in water, bring to boil, simmer for 25 minutes. Drain and arrange in one layer in an ovenproof dish.

In a small saucepan, heat butter, maple syrup, and brown sugar, bring to boil, simmer for 3–5 minutes, then pour over the potatoes, and bake for 45 minutes in a 350°F (180°C) oven. In the last 15 minutes, you can add orange juice, rum, and marshmallows. Serve with turkey.

Punkin Pie

This was the recipe Rosa made when Anthony said he wanted some "punkin pie" in the summer.

This was the recipe Tatiana made when Alexander said, hmm, I wouldn't mind some pumpkin pie tonight. In twenty minutes of prep, an hour of baking, and maybe half hour of cooling, he would be eating the pie with a spoon right out of the pie dish while she would be muttering, "Wait for the whipped cream. Wait for the whipped cream."

Crust:

1¼ cup (110g) finely crumbled graham crackers or other semi-sweet biscuits
¼ cup (50g) sugar
3 tablespoons butter, melted

Pumpkin Filling:

15oz (425g) canned pumpkin purée or cooked, mashed pumpkin
2 eggs
¼ cup (50g) sugar
⅛ teaspoon ground nutmeg
⅛ teaspoon ground cinnamon
1 cup (225ml) heavy cream

Preheat oven to 375°F (190°C) 20 minutes before cooking.

In a small bowl combine the graham crackers with the sugar and melted butter and mix through thoroughly. Press mixture into a pie dish with your fingers, pressing down hard and shaping it three-quarters up the sides.

In a medium bowl, beat pumpkin purée with eggs, sugar, nutmeg, and cinnamon.

In another medium bowl, whip heavy cream until stiff peaks form, and fold into pumpkin mixture. Pour filling into crust. Bake for 45 minutes or until toothpick inserted off the center comes out clean. Cool before serving with whipped cream. It might not last until it's cool. Refrigerate leftovers.

But after punkin pie, after sweet potatoes, after bacon and leek stuffing, after a month of playing in the snow and living with Aunt Esther, it was time to go. It was time to live on their own, time to make it on their own. Time for Tatiana to cook for her family again.

CHAPTER SEVEN

Miami by the Sea

After they had a place to hang their hat and Tatiana could cook for him again, she kept asking if she could make him lazy cabbage. But he kept saying no.

"Please don't make cabbage, Tania."

"What about cabbage pie?"

"No," said Alexander. "No more cabbage pie for us."

She wanted to cry. "But we cook potatoes," she tried.

"So? And what do potatoes have to do with anything?"

"What does cabbage?"

"I can't explain. You wouldn't understand."

She understood. With a bowed and saddened head, she understood. Things happened to him at war that forever changed things.

In the warmth of the azure sea and the humid air, far away from the memories of ice and snow, though, as it turned out, not far away enough, Tatiana had a houseboat she could call her own, with a tiny oven in which she could make some of the things she thought her war-torn husband might like. He worked all day on the Miami boats while she played with Anthony and thought up things to cook for him that might make him happy. He was always hungry, he always ate. He was gaining a little weight, wasn't looking as gaunt. Day by day, night by night, little by little, she tried restoring him. And restoring him was thus restoring her.

It was hot and moist all the time. Tatiana made salads to fit the climate, even though Alexander would eat the salad, and then say, "Okay, where's the food?" Tatiana learned to make a mango and feta cheese salad. Mangos were something she hadn't had before. The combination of sweet mangoes and slightly spicy feta was exotic, decidely un-Russian, decidedly un-cabbage-pie-like. She used cherry tomatoes halved, a mango cubed, a little red onion minced, and feta crumbled. She dressed it with lime and honey and a pinch of salt. She loved it. He ate it. "Where's the food?" he said.

In Coconut Grove, Tatiana discovered plantains. She chose her plantains wisely. They were ripe when they had black vertical marks in the yellow skin. They took longer to ripen than regular bananas, and thus kept longer.

She would slice two ripe plantains into ¼-in pieces and fry them on medium heat in 3 tablespoons of butter until they were golden brown, then lowering the heat to finish cooking through. She would serve them with anything, but mostly with skirt steak or fish; or, at the end of a meal, with rum, which flowed freely from the sugar-cane country of Cuba, just south of their houseboat on the Bay of Biscayne.

Challah Rolls

Her oven was an underperformer, which made it difficult to make bread. She tried challah rolls, which she had learned how to make from the Jewish women on the Lower East Side. She would make the small sweet rolls and fill them with ham or thinly sliced beef, and bring them for lunch with her when she ran to pick up Anthony from the boat in the afternoons. The three of them would sit under the palms. Tatiana would eat half a sandwich, Anthony would eat the other half and Alexander would devour three or four, and still look slightly searching when he was done. He liked them warm, so she made them every other morning, and brought them to him fresh. One evening he said, "Hey, you don't have any more of those little rolls, do you?" She did, and he piled his cod with mango salsa on top of them, and ate his haute cuisine seafood on a sandwich roll from the Lower East Side. On Sundays, he had them in the morning with his eggs and bacon. He had them with everything. Anthony was sick of them. Tatiana was sick of them. Not Alexander. And she didn't question it. He was eating. And who would want to question why the husband liked warm sweet bread right out of the oven?

Making yeast dough was time consuming, and yet bread was perishable. The inclination was to double the recipe, but bread went stale fast. Tatiana was lucky to have the morning to herself when Anthony was on the boat with Alexander, so that she could run to the market, do the laundry, and make him the bread he liked best.

The recipe made eighteen challah rolls. In Tatiana's houseboat, eighteen rolls lasted twenty-four hours. On the second day, she popped them in the oven for a few minutes to warm them up before making Alexander's lunch. They still tasted pretty good but not like the first day.

Yeast:

4 teaspoons dried yeast
1 cup (225 ml) very warm water
1 teaspoon sugar

Dough:

4½ cups (560 g) bread flour or all-purpose (plain) flour
3 eggs
½ cup (100g) sugar
⅛ cup (30ml) honey
½ cup (125 ml) canola oil
2 teaspoons salt
1 egg, beaten, for brushing
butter, for greasing

Glaze:

1 egg yolk
2 tablespoons melted butter
2 tablespoons water

To prove the yeast: combine yeast, water and sugar in small bowl, set aside in a warm place for ten minutes until frothy.

Meanwhile in a stand mixer with the dough hook attachment, combine flour, eggs, sugar, honey, oil, and salt, mix, and then knead for 10 minutes until the dough is smooth and sticky. Grease a large bowl with butter. Place dough into bowl and turn several times until buttered on all sides. Cover the bowl with a towel or plastic wrap (clingfilm) and place in a warm, dark place to rise for 90 minutes. Punch down, cover, let rise for another 45 minutes. Separate dough into halves, separate each half into thirds. Roll out each third into a rope about 18 in (45 cm) long. Tie the three ropes at the top and braid down. Cut into nine equal parts. Place on greased cookie sheet (baking tray). Repeat with the other half of the dough. Let the rolls rise another 45 minutes. Prepare egg glaze: egg yolk, 2 tablespoons melted butter, 2 tablespoons water, mix well, then brush over the rolls. Bake in a 360°F (190°C) oven for 30 minutes until rich golden brown. Cool on a wire rack.

Cod or Mahi-Mahi with Mango Salsa

Tatiana sometimes used papaya or ripe pineapples instead of mango but liked mango best. She was careful not to substitute a whole pineapple in place of a whole mango. For this she measured: 1 cup (150g) diced mango = 1 cup (150g) diced papaya or pineapple.

Mango Salsa:

- 3 tablespoons fresh lemon juice
- 3 tablespoons fresh lime juice
- 1 teaspoon grated lemon zest
- 1 mango, peeled, seeded and finely chopped
- 1 small tomato, finely chopped
- ⅓ cup (50g) red onion, finely chopped and lightly cooked so it's wilted and transparent
- 1 garlic clove, finely chopped
- 1 tablespoon honey
- ½ small jalapeño pepper, seeded and minced (very finely chopped)
- 2 tablespoons chopped fresh cilantro (coriander)

Since the fish takes only a few minutes, prepare the mango salsa first. Combine all ingredients in order, add honey, mix well, then sprinkle jalapeño and cilantro on top. Set aside.

4 fillets cod or Mahi-Mahi
3 tablespoons butter
1 tablespoon olive oil
salt, to taste

In a skillet heat oil and butter, add Mahi-Mahi, fry for 5 minutes on one side, till lightly brown, 5 minutes on the other. Serve with mango salsa.

And plantains.

Marinated Flank or Skirt Steak

When Alexander came home and asked what was for dinner, and Tatiana said marinated flank steak or skirt steak, he would nod approvingly. "Now that's what I call dinner. Not that food you call salad and I call rabbit food. Rabbits eat salad. And then I eat the rabbit. Any more challah rolls left?"

Steak was his favorite. He ate the salad, the salsa, the plantains, anything, as long as he had steak with it. "Where did you learn the marinade? It's great."

"From Chang Hao."

"Oh, your little Oriental friend. Did he want to marry you, too? To un-widow you?"

"No, Shura. Chang Hao had a wife."

"Oh, sure. So you say."

He was teasing her!

¼ cup (55 ml) soy sauce
¼ cup (55 ml) rice vinegar
2 teaspoons sugar
¼ cup (55 ml) red wine

Marinate steak for an hour or more in the above ingredients. But 15 minutes is better than nothing. Tatiana would sometimes marinate all day.

"That Chang Hao," Alexander said, finishing off second, third helpings. "He clearly was a superior teacher."

Stuffed Shells on the Stove

Sometimes Tatiana's restorative measures took a step back. Stuffed cabbage was such a time. She just couldn't leave it alone.

1941:

"Tania, can you make stuffed cabbage for dinner tomorrow?"

"Of course, Alexander. If there is meat in the stores, I will try."

1947:

"Please, Shura, please. Can I make stuffed cabbage for dinner tomorrow?"

"No, Tania."

"But your son loves it so much."

"No, Tania. He loves bread pudding, too. Make that instead." He retreated into silence and cigarettes again. Why did she have to open her mouth?

She stopped asking.

Tatiana did not make stuffed cabbage again until Alexander went to Vietnam in 1969—but by then, Anthony, the boy who had loved stuffed cabbage was also gone, and her other children, having never seen meat wrapped inside a cabbage, refused to eat it. She ate it by herself over a course of several days, and then threw the rest out, retreating into silence while remembering a life long gone, and living in dread fear for the present life that felt as if it might also soon be gone.

Anthony didn't need restoring. His mother was back; he spent every day with her. They were at the beach and on the swings all day. And in the mornings, he went with his dad on the boats. Anthony wore his cap and tried to be very serious, like his dad. He watched him to imitate him, he tried to deepen his voice, to slow it down, to stop it from inflecting, so he could sound like his dad. And when his dad was silent, as he was so often, Anthony was silent, too.

"Daddy wasn't always like that, honey," Tatiana said to Anthony one late afternoon when they had been on the beach playing. Anthony had asked her if Dad had forgotten most of his English perhaps, having been away so long. Had he forgotten Russian, too?

"He hasn't forgotten. He is just thinking things."

"Like what?"

"I don't know." Tatiana wasn't about to tell a four-year-old the truth. "Maybe he's thinking he is hungry. Or maybe he is thinking he is tired."

"He seems sad," declared Anthony.

And that's when Tatiana said that he wasn't always like that. "He used to be a kid, like you, Ant. He used to run, and play ball, and chase me."

"Dad used to *chase* you?" Anthony couldn't believe it.

"Yes. We want to get him like that again."

"Yes," said Ant. And the next morning, on the boat with Alexander, waiting for the first wave of people to come, he said, "Dad, what kind of food do you like?"

"Food? Well, I like all kinds, bud."

"Everything?"

"No, not everything. You know I don't like cabbage."

Now it was Anthony's turn to hang his head. He loved cabbage.

"Mommy can cook other things you like. I like everything else Mommy feeds us."

"Mommy is the best cook in the world."

"Yes, she is."

"Vikki is a terrible cook."

"Not everyone's perfect, bud."

"But what do you really like? Really, really?"

Alexander contemplated. "I really like stuffed shells."

"Stuffed shells? Like Isabella made that one time for you?"

"Yes."

"Hmm."

When Alexander came home that evening from his afternoon run on the boat, he asked what they were having.

"Stuffed shells," said Tatiana.

Alexander glanced over at Anthony who had an impenetrable look on his face. He stared back at his father, for a second, two, and then Alexander winked. Anthony tried to wink back. He scrunched up his face and winked with both eyes.

Because Tatiana learned from Isabella, and Isabella made her own ricotta, in Miami Tatiana made her own, with four parts milk and one part buttermilk. Years later, when they settled in Arizona, and ricotta cheese was hard to find, she continued to make her own. But store-bought is certainly less fuss.

Stuffed Shells:

5–6 cups (1.125–1.35 liters) simple pasta sauce (p.85),
    canned tomato sauce, or passata
1 tablespoon olive oil or butter, plus extra butter for coating
    pasta
1¼lb (570g) ground beef sirloin
1lb (450g) medium pasta shells
1lb (450g) ricotta
1½lb (700g) mozzarella
salt and pepper, to taste

Prepare simple pasta sauce.
In a large frying pan over medium-high heat, in 1 table-

spoon of olive oil or butter, fry the ground beef until completely cooked through, but not browned. Add salt and pepper to taste.

Par-boil the pasta shells in a large, heavy-bottom pot, drain, mix a little butter into the shells so they don't stick.

Meanwhile, grate the mozzarella cheese. Add the ground beef to the shells, stir, add the pound of ricotta, stir. Add three-quarters of the prepared sauce, stir. Add half the grated mozzarella, stir carefully, then add the rest, don't stir, but cover completely and heat through on medium-low heat until the mozzarella on top is melted and the sauce is bubbly.

Serve with garlic bread (p.87).

They fell away from the table. Alexander said, "I'm so full, I can't move."

Anthony said, "I'm so full, I can't move."

Alexander pushed his chair away. Anthony pushed his chair away. Alexander rubbed his stomach with the palms of his hands. Anthony rubbed his stomach with the palms of his hands. Alexander lit a cigarette, picked up the paper, but after a minute or two put it down. Anthony was still sitting across from him, looking into his own picture book—without a cigarette.

"Ant," said Alexander. "Let's go to the beach. I feel like swimming."

"Really?"

"Really. I'll teach you how to get away from the sharks."

"Whaaaaat?"

"Shura . . ."

Alexander continued undaunted. "Yes. You know how? I'll pretend to be a shark, I'll chase you, and you'll have to get away from me. It's early evening, prime shark feeding time in these waters. Okay? Let's go. The sharks are hungry, too. Tania, come. Where's your bathing suit?"

Shepherd's Pie

"Dad, Mom is going to make you shepherd's pie tonight," said Anthony. They were walking to the boat in the early morning. Anthony was running along, trying to keep up.

"She is? What is it?"

"I think you'll like it. Wait till tonight."

"OK, bud."

"Are we going to go swimming after dinner again?"

"Depends how good this shepherd's pie is." With one hand, Alexander hoisted Anthony up and ran with him the rest of the way.

That evening, Alexander tried shepherd's pie for the first time. Meat mixed with corn and carrots covered with a layer of mashed potatoes which were covered with a layer of cheese. There was nothing not to like.

"Tania, where'd you learn how to make this? Wait, let me guess," said Alexander. "From Chang Hao?" He was smiling.

Tatiana tutted.

Alexander laughed. She told him she had adjusted the recipe for beef instead of lamb, and for fresh meat instead of leftovers. "Good choice," said Alexander. "Well, Ant? Ready to go swimming?"

"Yes! But please. Don't be a shark today, Dad."

"All right, bud. Tonight the sharks are full."

¼ cup (50g) butter, or olive oil
1 medium onion, grated or very finely chopped
2 cloves garlic, grated very finely chopped
2lb (900g) ground beef sirloin
¼ cup (50g) tomato paste
6 tablespoons all-purpose (plain) flour
2 tablespoons Worcestershire sauce
2 tablespoons soy sauce
3 cups (675ml) beef stock
1 cup (225ml) red wine or beer
salt and pepper, to taste
3–4 carrots, peeled and thinly sliced
1 cup (165g) frozen corn kernels
4lb (1.8kg) mashed potatoes (p.132)
5oz (150g) sharp cheddar cheese, grated
5oz (150g) Monterey Jack or other hard mild cheese, grated
¼ cup (15g) breadcrumbs

In a large skillet heat butter or oil on medium-high, and brown onion for 3–4 minutes, and then garlic for 30 seconds. Add meat, brown. Turn heat down slightly, add tomato paste and flour and stir until fully absorbed into the meat. Add

Worcestershire sauce, soy sauce, beef stock and red wine, or beer, mix well, and simmer uncovered. Add carrots, simmer on low for 10 minutes, while you prepare the mashed potatoes. Add corn, stir, continue cooking. Add a little water, if necessary. The mixture should be thick and juicy but not runny. Preheat the oven to 350°F (180°C). Spoon mixture into a large casserole dish with deep sides. Arrange mashed potatoes on top, leveling off with a spatula. Sprinkle with grated cheese. Sprinkle with breadcrumbs. Bake for 30 minutes or until bubbly.

Chili

"Chili, Tania?"

"Chili, Alexander. With corn bread."

"Corn bread. Of course. Two things you like. Am I going to like this corn bread?"

"I think you're going to love it."

"Hmm. I think you're outdoing yourself."

"I don't see how that's possible. You won't let me cook anything I actually know how to cook."

"Yes, but look at the things you're cooking."

"Hmm. No Russian food."

"That's the point."

3 tablespoons olive oil
2 tablespoons butter

1 large onion, very finely chopped
3 garlic cloves, minced
2lb (900g) ground beef sirloin
salt, to taste
4 tablespoons chili powder
32oz (900g) canned red kidney beans, with juice
16oz (450g) canned tomato sauce, or 2 cups (450ml)
    passata
1 cup (225ml) water

To garnish:

8oz (225g) sharp cheddar cheese, grated
cilantro (coriander)
green (spring) or white onions, very finely chopped
sour cream
boiled white rice, to serve

Preheat heavy bottom 6-quart (4.5-liter) pan on medium.
Add olive oil and butter, heat for 2–3 minutes. Add onion,
cook until transparent and lightly golden. Add garlic, cook
for a minute, turn heat to medium-high, add sirloin, cook,
stirring and breaking up into little pieces, until cooked
through. Add salt, chili powder, stir, add kidney beans with
juices, tomato sauce, water, cover, cook for 20–30 minutes,
while the rice cooks.

Serve over white rice, topped with shredded cheese and, if
you like, onions, cilantro, and sour cream, with corn bread

on the side. Tatiana knew that some people skipped the rice and served chili right over the corn bread. But the bread was sweet, and the chili was savory. Alexander ate the chili over the rice *and* the corn bread.

Tania's Best Corn Bread

Moist, sweet, delicious. If you like corn bread, this is hard to beat. You can use all half-and-half instead of mixing with buttermilk, but Tatiana liked the slight acidity provided by the buttermilk. Serve to accompany chili.

1 cup (150g) all-purpose (plain) flour
1 cup (150g) corn meal
½ cup (100g) sugar
½ teaspoon salt
1 tablespoon baking powder
1 stick (110g) unsalted butter, softened, plus extra for greasing
1 egg
½ cup (125ml) half-and-half, or equal quantities of cream and
   milk
½ cup (125ml) buttermilk

Heat oven to 400°F (200°C). Lightly grease a 6-cup muffin tin.

In a medium bowl, combine the flours, sugar, salt and baking powder and mix well. Add butter and mix with a fork or a wooden spoon until mixture is crumbly.

In another bowl combine half-and-half, buttermilk and egg and whisk until combined. Add to the flour mixture, mix carefully with wooden spoon until just combined. Fill the muffin tins to the top. Bake 22 minutes or so until toothpick comes out clean. Do not overbake. Muffins will not get very brown on top. You can also make the corn bread in a cast-iron pot in the oven, or cast-iron corn bread molds.

Anthony for a long while ate nothing but corn bread.

Many evenings they went swimming and to the park, and Alexander every once in a while even chased Tatiana into the water and over the monkey bars.

After the corn bread when they went to the beach, and Anthony found a little friend to dig sand holes with, Alexander and Tatiana played in the water, she was swimming away, he was catching up with her, just because she had gotten a fair jump and was far ahead. He yelled after her, "Watch out, Tania, because when I capture you tonight, I warn you, I take no prisoners."

Promise, Shura? she whispered to herself, slowing down so he could catch her.

Plantains with Rum

They took a short walk at night to the park near their houseboat after Anthony fell asleep. They walked side by side. Tatiana noticed that he slowed down so that she could keep up with him. He walked close, and his bare arm bumped against her bare arm. They walked like this in the warm silence, and then Alexander reached down and took hold of Tatiana's hand. She squeezed back, she held her breath.

"Tatia . . ." he whispered.

"Yes, darling?"

"Oh, nothing. When we come back, can you make that dessert I like?"

"You'll have to be more specific. Bread pudding?"

"Plantains with rum."

"Ah. Of course. Want to go back now? I'll make it right away."

"No, not yet. Let's just . . . walk a while. Not too far. The boy will be fine. He never wakes up." He saw her face. "Never wakes up until we're right in the middle of something."

"Yes. Sleep."

"Come on. Just to the water. I'll have a smoke. Then we'll go back."

They walked in silence the rest of the way to the picnic benches under the palm trees, the Biscayne Bay a dark breath away. He lit a cigarette. She climbed on the table and sat next to him. They faced the water, sat quietly, didn't speak much.

"Your hair smells nice," he said, and, leaning over, lightly pressed his face into it.

Under the palms they sat, side by side, in the warm night that smelled of the salt ocean. He smoked. She inhaled for the Atlantic, for the Marlboro, for his breath, for his smell. She inhaled for everything. When he finished his cigarette, he glanced over at her. She glanced up at him, swallowed, and then carefully climbed into his lap.

"Just like before, huh, Tatiasha?" His arms went around her. He closed his eyes.

"Shh. Nothing is like before." She pressed his face into her neck, into her silken hair.

Plantains with Rum:

2–3 ripe plantains
3 tablespoons butter
¼ cup (50g) light brown sugar
¼ cup (60ml) rum
½ cup (110ml) heavy cream
Optional:
vanilla ice cream, to serve

Peel the plantains and cut them into ½-in (1cm) slices. Melt the butter in a heavy-bottom saucepan, add the plantains and cook for 5 minutes, turning over once, until both sides are light golden. Add sugar, mix, cook for another 3 minutes or so, until the plantains have absorbed the sugar.

Stir in the rum, light a match and ignite. The flame will be quite dramatic, small children will be both mortified and delighted. The husband will be horrified. Before he has time to start yelling and heading for the fire extinguisher, the flambé will be out. Remove from heat, stir in heavy cream, serve immediately, with ice cream if you wish.

CHAPTER EIGHT

Scottsdale in the Desert

Tatiana and Alexander settled in Arizona like immigrants piling out of their covered wagons. For a long time they lived *in* the covered wagon, so to speak, cooked on the fire outside and washed in the proverbial river. They lived as if they could not believe their good fortune. And then a remarkable thing happened, and so slowly that it went almost unnoticed by everyone. Tatiana got Le Creuset pots and Global knives. She bought Kitchen-Aid stand mixers and food processors, and Cuisinart baking utensils, cookie sheets and cheesecake forms. She filled her little kitchen with the products of permanence, and it was as if the utensils themselves sprouted into the ground and grew roots. When events conspired to make Alexander want to leave Arizona, Tatiana could not imagine leaving. This was home, for good, for bad, for ever.

In Arizona her cooking had changed once again. For one, Alexander bought a barbecue grill. Ever the soldier, he still liked cooking over an open flame, but now the open flame had a cast-iron rack and adjustable temperature and a warming tray. So the things that they cooked when they camped in the United States for three years became a fixture of their evenings—hamburgers, hot dogs, steak, chicken, sausage, baked potatoes, corn.

And Tatiana became friends with Francesca.

Francesca was a young woman from Mexico who lived down the street. For the first few years of their friendship, Francesca was always pregnant. During this time, Tatiana taught Francesca English and to return the favor, Francesca taught Tatiana how to cook some Mexican dishes. Tatiana never did make her own tortillas, but Alexander fully embraced the marinated steak called fajitas, and the lime chicken and the meatball soup, but none so much as the beergaritas, which he himself made every Saturday night, making every Saturday night a celebration, particularly if Anthony was sleeping over his friend Sergio's house, and Tatiana and Alexander were alone. Alexander had his own theory about beergaritas that he, for fear of offending Tatiana, did not verbalize unless she had some beergaritas in her, and then he hoped that by morning she wouldn't remember what he had called them: the reason Francesca kept having all those babies.

To go with Alexander's barbecues, Tatiana added more cold salads to their meals, not mayonnaise-based Russian salads, but lettuce and tomato based American salads.

And Tatiana baked. She baked cookies and corn muffins, banana bread and pies. The interest in baking never waned, because just as Anthony got to be a teenager and started to pretend he wasn't interested in his mother's cookies anymore, Tatiana had three more children, one after the other, first the two boys, sixteen months apart, and then a few years later a baby girl. So the sixties were spent waiting for letters from Anthony in Vietnam and baking for the little ones. And when the children grew up and had their own children, she baked for her grandchildren. No one could come to her house without asking if there was something she had made earlier that day. Everyone had their favorites, and Tatiana baked happily for them all, never denying them, for she always remembered the days spent on her hands and knees on the floor, licking the crumbs of the old stale oat flour out of a canvas bag, and wishing not for crumb cake or croissants but for no one in her family to come into the hallway because then she would have to share the scraps.

Arizona was too hot for soups, for stews, for a broiling kitchen. In the wintertime, Tatiana still made pot roast and curry and shepherd's pie but "winter" lasted from December to January, and early December still had apricot globemallow blooming on the lawns, and late January often had violet verbena peeking through the sand.

During their first eight years when Tatiana was working late at the hospital, there was no time to come home at eight and involve herself with an hour's worth of food prep. She made her food on the weekends and on her days off, so all Alexander had to do was preheat the oven, or put it on low on the stove. On her days off she cooked like a Saturday night short-order cook to make up to Alexander for her late hours at Phoenix Memorial. She thought food would soften him. Sometimes it did. Gradually, nothing would soften him, until life ultimately reached critical mass and exploded.

And then rebuilding bombed-out cities took, among other things, Tatiana making three children and Alexander building them a new home. Alexander would come home early from work and grill. She marinated the chicken and the steak for his grilling, she made the baked potatoes and the salads; they sat outside and drank cold liquids, they had steak with salad, and it was still light out, not dark, not cold. Winter seemed to disappear altogether when the new house was built, all white and sunny and spotless. In that house, it was always summer. And in that house, Tatiana made dessert and babies and then dessert *with* her babies in the white limestone-floor kitchen, while Alexander cooked the steak on the fire outside. "Like a soldier in the woods," Tatiana said.

"Just like that," said Alexander. "Except there was no meat, and we couldn't start a fire. But I know what you mean. Are you going to make your little rabbit food to go along with my actual food that I'm about to rip off the bone with my teeth?"

So Tania made her little rabbit food to go with his actual food. She made a salad with fresh mozzarella and bacon pieces. She used iceberg lettuce, cucumbers, sliced carrots, a tomato, crisp crumbled bacon (of course!) and fresh mozzarella, cut into small cubes. If she wanted to be adventurous, instead of mozzarella she used Gorgonzola cheese. "Why Gorgonzola?" asked Alexander. "For a little adventure," replied Tatiana. And he would stare at her for a second or two before saying, "It's a fine day indeed when using moldy cheese has become your idea of adventure. Why don't you really take risks and use two garlic cloves instead of one?"

For dressing, Tatiana made her own by combining ½ cup of olive oil, ½ cup of balsamic vinegar, *two* finely chopped garlic cloves, salt and pepper, one teaspoon of freshly squeezed lemon, and shaking very well before pouring.

Beef Tenderloin

Alexander called this "the king of meals." Tatiana cooked it only for guests she was trying to impress. The family loved this cut and had it often, and one afternoon, Harry's best friend and his parents came over for drinks and salsa, and as they were sitting on the deck, Harry asked, "Mom, what are we having for dinner?" and Tatiana, shrugging, said, "I don't know. What day is it? Monday? Filet mignon maybe?"

And the nearby Janie snorted and said, "Oh, no! Not again."

3–5lb (1.35–2.25kg) whole and uncut beef tenderloin,
 trimmed of fat

Marinade:

5 tablespoons butter, melted
2 teaspoons coarse salt
½ teaspoon freshly ground pepper
½ teaspoon cayenne or Cajun seasoning
2 garlic cloves, grated
1 tablespoon soy sauce
1 tablespoon rice vinegar
1 tablespoon red wine
1 teaspoon sugar

Leave tenderloin out at room temperature for 45 minutes.

Tie it with string from one end to the other, tie it in a spiral as if you were imprisoning it. Preheat oven to 450°F. On the stove top, heat 3 tablespoons peanut oil in a large roaster.

Prepare your marinade:

Whisk together the melted butter, salt, pepper, cayenne, garlic, soy sauce, vinegar, red wine, and sugar. Rub the marinade thoroughly over the tenderloin, then place in the preheated roaster on top of the stove and brown on medium-high 2 minutes on each side until nice and brown. Place on a rack inside the pot you just cooked it in, and grill inside the oven for 25 minutes. Take it out, let stand for 20 minutes to compose. It will become very moist and be much easier to slice.

In the winter, Tatiana served the tenderloin with mashed potatoes.

In the summer, Alexander grilled potatoes brushed with melted butter and left untouched on a closed medium grill for an hour. And because it was Tatiana's favorite, he grilled a sweet potato for her, while she melted a little butter with brown sugar and cinnamon to pour over the top.

Beef Barley Soup

Alexander's favorite soup.

Sirloin steak, onion, bay leaf, a little oregano, frozen mixed veg, water, a beef bouillon cube, barley, cooked for an hour. "It's almost like a Russian soup, Tatia," he would say, sitting at her table, and drawing the bowl near.

"Just the barley, Shura. No stringbeans in Russia, no corn."

"Yes, and no frozen veg."

"Well, no. And no olive oil. And no meat."

"Right. But the barley *is* Russian. The barley and the bay leaf."

"Yes, darling," said Tatiana. "It's almost like a Russian soup, then."

3 tablespoons olive oil
1 large onion, very finely chopped
2 garlic cloves, very finely chopped
1½lb (700g) sirloin steak, trimmed of fat and cut into 1-in (2.5cm) cubes
5 cups (1.125 litres) cold water
1 bay leaf
2 beef bouillon cubes
1 cup (175g) frozen mixed vegetables
½ cup (100g) pearl barley
salt and pepper, to taste

Heat the olive oil in a 4- or 5-quart (3.6- or 4.5-liter) pot, add onion, cook until pale, add garlic, cook 30 seconds, add cubed beef and brown on all sides for 5 minutes. Add water, bay leaf, salt, pepper, bouillon cubes, bring to boil, reduce heat, cover, simmer for 30 minutes. Add vegetables and barley, bring back to boil, reduce heat, cover and simmer 30 more minutes, or until barley is completely cooked.

Corn on the Cob

Corn was like plantains. Corn was quintessentially American. It was indigenous to the continent, the world had not heard of it until Christopher Columbus discovered it, it was not widely available elsewhere, and it was nearly completely unavailable in Russia, though they did have a name for it—"KookooROOza"—a made-up name for something they read about, like prairies and lassoes, but had never seen in real life. Tatiana's feeling for corn was strong. She made corn fritters, which were pancakes with corn, and corn muffins, which were muffins with corn meal, and corn chowder, which was soup with corn. And the children loved cornflakes and popcorn, and sometimes spent whole dinners wondering about the surprise and joy of the first Indian who placed a kernel over heat and kept it there long enough to pop and have a white puff, like cotton, pop out.

Alexander, amused by Tania's love for corn, prepared it in the simplest American way: he basted it with butter and placed it on his grill for five minutes, turning it over a few times. A few times, too, he called his grill the "*bourzhuika*" but this made Tatiana cry so he stopped doing it, but Tatiana said she knew he was thinking it, and cried anyway.

Tatiana cooked the corn in a little boiling water with the lid closed to let the steam take care of things. She added a teaspoon of sugar, and cooked it for only a few minutes because it was meant to be crunchy and sweet.

Onions, Onions, Onions

To everything Tatiana cooked, she added onions. Alexander said it was a Russian thing. "Can't take the Soviet Union out of the girl," he said.

"I don't know why you're complaining," she rejoined, chopping, mincing, slicing, frying. "You love onions. Think of your beef barley soup."

"I'm not complaining. I'm just saying."

She sliced them thinly and fried them on medium with butter and a little oil, she added salt and a little cayenne pepper when they got golden, and continued to fry until they caramelized. She used them in everything.

"Everything?" she asked. "Brownies?"

"Savory, I said."

"You didn't say."

At dinnertime, the house was first filled with the smell of bread, then the smell of onions, followed by the smell of chocolate.

Onions for flavor: stews, soups, sauces, and of course, macaroni and cheese.

"Of course," said Alexander. "Macaroni and cheese."

Onions sweet and caramelized, in hamburgers, over rice, over chicken, over steak. She just cut them differently. She small-diced them for hamburgers, but over steak or calves liver she sliced them thinly, julienne-style, in long strips.

For parties Tatiana made onion dip. Even her guacamole was passed up.

Onion Dip:

2 large onions, thinly sliced
2 tablespoons canola oil
2 tablespoons butter
¼ teaspoon cayenne pepper
½ teaspoon salt
½ teaspoon black pepper
½ cup (110g) mayonnaise
½ cup (110g) sour cream
½ cup (110g) cream cheese, at room temperature

Fry the onions on medium-high in the oil and butter. Reduce heat to medium-low, add cayenne pepper, salt, black pepper, continue to cook for 15 more minutes until caramelized. Don't stir for the first 7 minutes, and only occasionally afterwards. Make sure not to burn the onions, otherwise they lose their sweet taste and caramelized brown hue. Take off heat, cool slightly.

Meanwhile, mix together mayo, sour cream, and cream cheese, add onions with all the juices, mix well, serve warm. You can omit the cayenne pepper if you don't like kick in your onion dip. Alexander liked kick.

Guacamole

"Tania, you know what you haven't made in a while?"

They were sitting by the pool as the sun was setting. The children were jumping off the diving board—Tatiana would have liked to say one at a time, but it would not have been true.

"What haven't I made in a while? Corn?"

"No, you've made plenty of that. Francesca's guacamole."

Tatiana pondered. It was true, but why? "Well," she said at last, "we haven't had anyone over on the weekends recently, and the kids hate guacamole."

"This is true," said Alexander. "But you know who doesn't hate guacamole?"

"Um—you?"

"That's right."

"And me. So, OK, I make guacamole tonight."

"Good. And I'll get Harry to eat it. And if he eats it, Pasha will eat it. And if they eat it, Janie will eat it because she wants to be a boy."

"Um—do you need to be a boy to eat guacamole?"

"Tania."

"OK, OK, I'm going."

Anthony was not home anymore. He was in Vietnam.

169

Avocado should not be too mushy, nor too hard. It should feel springy when touched, like a peeled orange. If it feels like a walnut, don't buy, if it feels like a mashed mango, don't buy.

2 ripe, slightly softened avocados
2–3 tablespoons very finely chopped red onion
1 large garlic clove, grated
juice of ½ lime
3 tablespoons very finely chopped cilantro (coriander), or to taste
salt, to taste
1 small red tomato, finely chopped

Cut the avocados in half, scoop out the pit, then scoop the meat into a mortar. Add minced onion, garlic, lime juice, cilantro, salt and tomato. Mash coarsely with a pestle, making sure to leave some chunks.

Sure enough, when the guacamole was brought out, eight-year-old Harry dipped in his tortilla chip and ate it, alongside his dad. Pasha watched for a little while, uncertainly, but his mother, his father, and now his youngest brother were eating it. Clearly he had no choice. He dipped his chip in.

"I want some!" whined Janie. And she had some, too.

"How did you get Harry to eat it?" Tatiana later asked.

"Simple," said Alexander. "I told him it's what his dad lived on when he was in the forests of war-torn Europe."

"Shura! It's a sin to lie to your children."

"No, it isn't."

"Someday he'll find out you didn't know what an avocado was in the forests of Europe."

"My work by then will be done." Pause. "You know what else you haven't made in a while?"

"What, my love? *Blinchiki? Pirozhki?* Cabbage Pie? I haven't made that in fifteen years."

Alexander would not be baited. "No. Salsa."

"Salsa?"

"Yes. Salsa, with cream cheese on the side."

Salsa

3 ripe tomatoes, finely diced
½ jalapeño chili, seeded, and very finely chopped
4 tablespoons fresh cilantro (coriander), chopped
2 garlic cloves, very finely chopped
¼ red, Vidalia or other sweet onion, very finely chopped
juice of 1 lime
salt, to taste

Combine all ingredients and mix well. Serve with chips and cream cheese on the side.

Meatball Soup

Francesca taught Tatiana meatball soup. When Tania made the meat filling for *blinchiki*, she made the soup at the same time.

It went nicely with *blinchiki* or *pirozhki*. Even Francesca thought so, and she had previously had meatball soup only when accompanied by fajitas. So Francesca and Tatiana decided that meatball soup can be Russian *and* Mexican. It was inter-cuisinary.

When Tatiana cooked just for Alexander, Anthony, and herself it was easy to make plenty. But after Pasha and Harry were born, and after Janie, she had to ration the meatballs to the children, because there was no amount she could make that could fit in the pot that would be enough for them. No matter how many she made, they consumed them all.

Broth:

8 cups (1.8 liters) cold water
1 large onion, peeled and left whole
3 garlic cloves, sliced crossways
16oz (450g) canned peeled whole tomatoes
salt and pepper, to taste
¼ cup fresh cilantro (coriander)
4 medium potatoes, peeled and cubed
4 carrots, peeled and thinly sliced

Meatballs

2lb (900g) ground beef sirloin
½ cup (95g) raw white rice
1 large onion, grated
2 garlic cloves, grated
½ cup (25g) breadcrumbs
salt and pepper, to taste

Fill a large pot with 8 cups (1.8 liters) water, and while bringing to boil, add onion, garlic, canned tomatoes, fresh cilantro, and salt and pepper, to taste. (Make sure the tomatoes are peeled, otherwise the tomato skins separate; since they don't soften, they're impossible to eat.)

Meanwhile in a large bowl combine ground sirloin and uncooked rice. Add grated onion, grated garlic, salt, pepper, and breadcrumbs, mix well.

Make the meatballs. Drop them into the boiling broth. Bring back to boil, cover, lower heat, and simmer for 45 minutes. Add potatoes and carrots, bring back to boil, lower heat, simmer for 30 minutes or until the vegetables are soft. Adjust seasoning as necessary. You can serve this soup with *blinchiki*, but it's like a meal in itself.

Fajitas

Alexander called Tatiana a cooking chameleon. Just as Leningrad cooking had Russian influence, and lower New York cooking had Isabella's Italian influence, and Esther's cooking had the American, New England Pilgrim influence, so Arizona's cooking was stamped with Francesca's Mexican roots.

The sainted Francesca taught Tatiana fajitas. "For señor Alexander," she said. "He will like."

"Oh, yes, he will, Francesca," said Tatiana.

She taught Tatiana this, and meatball soup. Both became a staple in the Barrington household.

1½–2lb (700–900g) flank, skirt or blade steak
juice of 2 limes
3 garlic cloves, very finely chopped
1 medium onion, thinly sliced
5 tablespoons olive oil, for frying
½ teaspoon ground cumin
4 tablespoons chopped cilantro (coriander)
1 green or red pepper (capsicum), seeded, and thinly sliced
Optional:
half a small jalapeño chili, coarsely chopped. Jalapeño is very
spicy, be careful not to touch your eyes as you chop it. Tatiana
once tasted the marinade and then, in a fit of affection, kissed
Alexander's eyes. He was not happy.

Slice the steak against the grain into long strips ½ in (1cm) wide. Place in a large bowl, add other ingredients, mix and marinate, the longer the better, overnight is ideal.

Heat a heavy-bottom skillet on medium-high, add 3 tablespoons olive oil, add steak, and fry for 5–7 minutes, turning over after 4 minutes, until well-browned on all sides, but still pink inside. Cook on higher heat if you want it less cooked inside, but still nicely browned on the outside. Remove meat from heat, add remaining 2 tablespoons olive oil, add the onion and green pepper from the marinade, drain of liquid, and cook on high heat for 2–3 minutes until sizzling brown.

Serve fajitas with refried beans, guacamole, salsa, grated cheese (Monterey Jack or mild cheddar), sour cream, and warm tortillas.

Oh, and lime and cilantro rice.

Lime and Cilantro Rice

5 cups (1.25 liters) chicken stock
½ cup (110ml) white wine
juice of 2 limes
2 tablespoons olive oil
1 small onion, very finely chopped
½ teaspoon salt
pepper, to taste
1 cup (200g) long-grain or basmati rice
2 garlic cloves, very finely chopped

2 tablespoons butter
2 tablespoons fresh cilantro (coriander), chopped
Optional:
1 cup (225g) grated Monterey Jack or other hard, mild cheese

In a medium saucepan, bring chicken stock, white wine, and juice of limes to a boil, reduce heat. Meanwhile, in a large, heavy-bottom skillet heat olive oil on medium-high, add onion, cook, stirring constantly for a few minutes. Add salt, pepper, and stir. Add rice, coat well, add garlic, stir and cook for another half a minute. Add the lime-wine stock, stir well, cover, lower heat to medium and cook for 15 minutes until liquid is absorbed and rice is tender. Remove from heat, add butter and cilantro, stir, serve. Sprinkle cheese on top without stirring through.

Cajun Chicken with Lime

Lime is like cilantro, Francesca taught Tatiana. You put it in beer, in tequila, over rice, in marinade, always on chicken. "And when you have a headache, rub a little lime juice on your forehead."

"On your forehead, really?"

"Really."

Alexander had walked into the kitchen. "Francesca, do you really need lime on your forehead after all that lime-infused tequila? I think intravenous lime will have probably done the trick, no?"

"What he say?" Francesca asked Tatiana. "I tell by his face he teasing me, but what he say?"

4 garlic cloves, very finely chopped or grated
1 medium onion, sliced
juice of 1 lime
1½ cups (340ml) buttermilk. If you can't find buttermilk use yogurt
2 teaspoons salt
2 teaspoons Cajun seasoning
2lb (900g) thick chicken breast fillets

In a large mixing bowl combine all ingredients except the chicken. Add the chicken, mix thoroughly with the marinade. Cover with a small plate, put large weight on top: a 3lb (1.35kg) weight, a rock, a jar of pickles, etc. Marinate in the fridge for 4–8 hours.

The buttermilk makes the chicken unbelievably tender, and difficult to overcook. You can also marinate chicken breast on the bone, if you prefer.

To prepare for cooking, take chicken out of the marinade and pat dry with paper towels. To cook you have a few options: a) If it's summer, you can cube the chicken, thread onto skewers and grill on the barbecue for 2 minutes a side on medium, with the cover closed.

b) You can add vegetables or onions in between the chunks of chicken and make like a shish-ke-bob.

c) Or you can grill the chicken breasts whole on the barbecue.

Beergaritas

"Tania, it's Saturday night."

"Yes, so?"

"Anthony is asleep." It was just the three of them back then.

"Yes, so?"

"So, so. You know what time it is, don't you?"

"Tea time?"

"No."

"Um, bedtime?"

"Not quite." He grinned. "Beergarita time."

"Oh, *that* time."

> 1 12–16oz can frozen sweetened lime juice concentrate, such as Limeade
>
> 2 fresh limes, quartered
>
> 1¼ cups (275ml) Patron Reposado tequila
>
> 5oz (150ml) Triple Sec or Cointreau (you can try Grand Marnier but Tania finds it not sweet enough)
>
> 2 bottles Corona or Rolling Rock beer, or any lager beer of your choice
>
> Ice

In a large pitcher, combine all ingredients; except for the beer, stir well to mix. Add beer, serve. Tatiana doesn't recommend putting through a blender, the fizziness of the beer works against the taste, and she definitely doesn't recommend driving afterward. It's stunningly and deceptively potent. It tastes as if you're drinking a Corona with lime. And suddenly—you're acting silly and singing in Mexican. And when you say you don't know any Mexican, Tatiana says, that's exactly my point. More on that below:

Best Ever Rum Cake:

1 tablespoon sugar
1 cup (175g) dried fruit
1 teaspoon soda
2 large eggs
lemon juice
1 or 2 quarts (900ml or 1.8 liters) good, dark rum
1 cup (200g) brown sugar
1 cup (225g) butter
½ teaspoon baking powder
½ cup (50g) chopped walnuts (black if you can find 'em)

Select a large mixing bowl, measuring cup, etc. Before starting, sample the rum to check quality. Good, isn't it? Now proceed:

Check rum again, it must be just right. To be sure rum is the proper quality, pour one level cup of rum into a glass and drink it as fast as you can . . . good rum goes down smooth and easy. Bad rum won't. Repeat to make sure it is good quality.

With electric mixer, beat 1 cup of butter in a large fluffy bowl. Add 1 seaspoon of thugar and beat again. Meanwhile, make sure rum is still alright. Try another cup. Open second quart if necessary. Add leggs, 2 cups dried druit and beat till high. If druit gets stuck in beaters, pry loose with drewscriber. Sample rum again, checking for tonscisticity. Next sift 3 cups pepper or salt (really doesn't matter). Sample rum. Sift ½ pint lemon juice. Fold in chopped butter and strained nuts. Add 1 tablespoon of brown thugar—or whatever color you can find. Wix mell. Grease oven. Turn cake pan to 350 gradees. Pour mess into boven and ake. Check rum again and go to qed.

Banana Bread

When Tatiana first came to America, the bananas never ripened. They never ripened because she would eat them before they did. She bought them barely yellow and ate them barely yellow. She had never had bananas in the Soviet Union and now feasted on them the way she feasted on bacon. Then slowly, the bananas started hanging on the hook longer and longer, getting more yellow, getting black-pitted. She didn't like to eat them when they were overripe, so she started figuring out what else to do with them. She put them over her cold cereal, ate them with vanilla yogurt, mashed them and put them in her pancakes, and she dipped them in chocolate (20 oz (570g) melted chocolate chips, 1 stick (110g) melted butter) and called them chocolate covered bananas. She served them at barbecues with chocolate covered strawberries and they were the highlight of the party. But the bananas were still going too ripe. She could have just stopped buying them, but that was like saying she should stop making bread every other day. The bananas represented a different life. Bananas, plantains, sweet potatoes, corn, turkey were all symbols of the new world. So she bought them every time she bought milk, like a staple, and they hung on the hook. That's when Tatiana started making banana bread. She tinkered with this recipe, putting in too many eggs and too much flour, not enough sugar, not enough bananas. There was a period of months in the '50s when Alexander and Anthony ate banana bread every week. One took it to work, one took it to school. "Is it good?" she would ask them, and they would reply, "It is good."

She would pause. "Why don't you like it?"

"I like it," Alexander would say.

"No, you don't. I can tell by your face. Why are you reserved? Why don't you like it?"

"I'm not reserved. I like it."

The next day there would be new banana bread. "Try this. Maybe this is better. I put more sugar in."

Alexander would taste it. "It is good."

"Oh, no. Why don't you like it?"

And so it went. Still her boys took it with them, but finally, after some months, Tatiana figured it out.

"OK," she said. "Taste this."

Alexander tasted. "Oh my God."

"Ah. *Now* you like it."

And the irony was, once she figured it out, she stopped making it quite as often, but the irony was, once she figured it out, Alexander and Anthony couldn't stop asking for it.

This is that recipe.

Banana Bread:

1 stick (110g) butter, at room temperature

1 cup (200g) sugar, at room temperature (Ha!)

2 eggs, at room temperature

4 teaspoons fresh lemon juice

1 teaspoon grated orange zest

⅓ cup (75ml) water

1 teaspoon vanilla extract

4 very ripe bananas, mashed

1¾ cups (220g) all-purpose (plain) flour, sifted

1 teaspoon baking soda

½ teaspoon salt

Preheat oven to 350°F (180°C). Grease the bottom of a loaf or pound-cake pan. Cream butter and sugar in an electric mixer. Add eggs, lemon juice, orange rind, water, vanilla, and then the bananas. Mix thoroughly so the bananas become smooth, not chunky. In a separate bowl combine flour, baking soda and salt, and fold into the banana mixture on low until just mixed. Pour into the cake pan and bake for 45 minutes or until pick inserted just off center comes up clean. Leave for 5–10 minutes in pan, then turn out onto plate.

Optional:

add ½ cup (50g) chopped walnuts, or ½ cup (75g) chocolate chips. Or both. Everyone loves the chocolate chips.

Fudgy Chewy Brownies

Pasha tried to be stoic when it came to fudge brownies, but his undeniable weakness for them propelled him into his mother's kitchen where he would stand timidly near the mixer, pretending to be interested in just the ingredients that went into the batter. "How long do we have to beat the egg yolks for? Fifteen minutes? Wow. Why so long?" He watched the sugar, the eggs. He offered to help his mother melt the chocolate. He carried the melted chocolate to the refrigerator to cool it. He kept time, monitored the room temperatures of things. It was all with one goal in mind. To get the wooden spoon and the mixing bowl after the brownies went in the oven. Tatiana started leaving a little more in the bowl, to please her son. Then a little more. Eventually, it became clear: she had to double the recipe in order to please him completely and still have mixture left over for baking. When she doubled the recipe the rest of the children got to lick the bowl also. But no one enjoyed it as much as moderate, composed, not-easily-rattled Pasha. Harry and Janie and Alexander had other weaknesses; brownies were Pasha's.

The recipe called for semi-sweet chocolate and unsweetened chocolate. It was very good this way, very fudgy, very chocolatey. If you like your brownies slightly less intense, use milk chocolate instead of semi-sweet. Tatiana had great success using chocolate shavings made for hot chocolate, and unsweetened cocoa powder instead of the unsweetened chocolate blocks. Use according to your preference. Alexander liked them milky, Anthony and Harry liked them dark, and Pasha ate them any which way. Janie preferred them the opposite way to whoever was annoying her most at the moment. Tatiana was thus forced to make two batches, one milk, one dark. They rarely lasted through the evening.

1 cup (200g) sugar
2 eggs, at room temperature
⅛ teaspoon salt
6oz (175g) milk or semi-sweet chocolate
2oz (50g) unsweetened cocoa powder or unsweetened chocolate
½ cup (110g) unsalted butter
¼ cup (30g) all-purpose (plain) flour
1 teaspoon vanilla extract

In an electric mixer beat the sugar, eggs and salt for 13–16 minutes. Meanwhile in a double boiler, melt the chocolate and butter on low heat. When the chocolate is two-thirds melted, take off heat and melt fully by stirring. Cool to lukewarm before folding into the egg mixture. Then by hand with a wooden spoon, fold in flour and add vanilla. Pour into the prepared pan and bake for 20 minutes or until a toothpick inserted off the center comes up clean. Cool before serving. Cover and refrigerate leftovers. Serve them with cream cheese icing: 1 cup (125g) powdered (icing) sugar, 1 teaspoon vanilla extract, ½ cup (125g) cream cheese and ¼ cup (50g) butter, all at room temperature, all mixed well until smooth.

"Creature Cookies"

In the nineteenth century these cookies were called preacher cookies. They were called preacher cookies because when a woman looked outside her kitchen window and saw the minister walking down the hill toward her house, they could be ready for him by the time he reached her front door. Of course Harry, when he heard Mama was making preacher cookies heard "creature" cookies, so that's how they became known.

"Harry, you fool," Pasha said. "They're not called creature cookies. They're called *preacher* cookies."

"You're wrong," Harry stated flatly. "As always."

"Oh yeah? Then what are *creature* cookies made with?" Pasha said triumphantly.

"Oh yeah?" said an even more triumphant Harry. "You fool. Then what are *preacher* cookies made with?"

½ cup (110ml) milk
½ cup (110g) butter
2 cups (400g) sugar

Heat the milk with the butter and sugar until it comes to full boil. Reduce heat. Add:

3 cups (350g) quick-cook oats
½ cup (50g) unsweetened cocoa
1 teaspoon vanilla extract

And here you can also add:

½ cup (40g) shredded coconut or
½ cup (125g) chunky (crunchy) peanut butter or
½ cup (50g) chopped walnuts

Cook for about a minute, until thick and mushy. Take off heat, and spoon onto foil in little round teaspoon lumps. Cool to room temperature before eating.

Overcooking the oatmeal sometimes turns the creature cookies into chocolate hockey pucks, delicious but not for those with weak teeth. Or it turns them into boiled glue. Harry loves them either way, saying no one but a true lover of cookies made with creatures could eat them in this state.

Fruit Salad

The children helped Tatiana prepare for parties by making fruit salad. She agreed at first, thinking it would be fun for them, and they could sample the goods as they put them into a collective bowl. But in no time, the making of fruit salad devolved into the throwing of fruit salad. First, there was the inevitable argument as to what fruits actually qualified for inclusion. Janie wanted watermelon, but

Harry said no. He wanted grapes. Pasha said no grapes, but mangoes. Harry said no mangoes, but kiwi. Janie didn't know what kiwi was and said definitely no kiwi. The argument got heated, and instantly violent—toward the fruit. The watermelon, the kiwi, the grapes were all over the floor of Tatiana's kitchen, the children were thrown out and sent into the pool, and Tatiana made her own fruit choices. When the guests came, they said, oh what delicious fruit salad, and the three children, standing clean and proud and *so* well-behaved said, "Oh, thank you. We made it."

2 cups watermelon, cubed
2 cups strawberries, halved
1 cup blueberries
1 cup apples, peeled and cubed
2 cups green grapes

Or whatever fruit your family won't throw in your kitchen. Add ½ cup (110ml) orange juice, ½ cup (100g) sugar, mix well.

Lemon Chiffon Pie

Alexander loved all things lemon like lemon meringue pie and Tatiana for a long time made that, then found an easier method which made it even better. Alexander asked for it once a month in the summertime.

"Dad, is there anything Mommy makes that you don't love?" asked Harry.

"No, son," Alexander replied. "I eat and like everything your mommy gives me." He smiled—meant for Tatiana, not Harry.

"Come on—there is not *one* thing she makes that you don't like?"

"No, son."

Harry looked skeptical.

Pasha came in and snorted at his brother. "Harry, you're a primitive. What don't you understand? If Dad doesn't like it, Mom doesn't make it."

Harry's eyes widened. He was only six at the time; he didn't understand. "Is that true?"

Tatiana and Alexander said nothing.

"Go get the plates and forks for dessert," said Tatiana. And the lemon chiffon was served, and it was delicious. Everyone forgot for the moment the simple truth of things, the undeniable truth of things—that if Daddy didn't like it, Mommy didn't make it.

"Mommy, you are the bestest mommy in the world," said Janie, who was three. "There are other mommies, but there is no mommy bester than you."

Crust:

9-in (23cm) pie crust, store bought, or pre-made (p.50)
1 egg white, beaten

Filling:

15oz (425g) lemon curd
4 egg whites, at room temperature

½ teaspoon cream of tartar
⅓ cup (70g) sugar
powdered (icing) sugar, for sprinkling

Pre-bake the pie crust, with weights, for 20 minutes in a 425°F (220°C) oven. When it cools down slightly, brush with a little egg white. Reduce oven temperature to 375°F.

Meanwhile whip the other 4 egg whites until soft peaks form. Add cream of tartar, and then little by little the sugar. Fold carefully into lemon curd until just combined. Pour into pre-baked, still warm pie crust and bake for 20 minutes until lightly golden on top. When it cools completely, sprinkle with powdered sugar.

Marilyn's Lemon Whippersnappers

Alexander came home one evening from work, stuck something into Tatiana's mouth and said, "Here, try this."

She tried it. "Pretty good," she said. "Lemon?"

"Daddy, Daddy, I want some!" cried Janie. Alexander, denying his only daughter little, gave her one, then another.

"It's dinnertime, Shura," said Tatiana.

"Mommy, these are sooooo good," Janie said. Luckily the boys were outside playing basketball.

"All right, I'll bite," said Tatiana. "Where'd you get them?"

"Oh, it's a long story," Alexander replied, pretend-casual, pretend-dismissive.

"Turns out, I got nothin' but time," said Tatiana.

"Well, you know Shannon is building a custom gig on Shea, and the short version is, that there was a problem with the pitch of the roof, I came to help, we fixed it by putting a deck underneath to balance things out, and as a thank you, I got these cookies, from Marilyn, who's building the house with her husband, the superintendent of Scottsdale schools."

Tatiana looked singularly unimpressed with Marilyn's husband's respectable and handily tossed-about credentials. She said, "Hmm. So you got the cookies from Marilyn. What did Shannon get?"

"Nothing! I did most of the work."

"I see."

"They're good, aren't they?" Alexander grinned and scooped her up into his arms. "If I fix *your* roof and build you a deck, will you make them for me?"

"Shura, look, the kids . . ."

The kid, rather, *was* looking. But Alexander and Tatiana were kissing, and didn't care. Tatiana did make the lemon whippersnappers for him, and for Janie, and for Pasha and Harry. They inhaled them, and said, if only Ant were here, he'd love them. He loves lemon—like Dad.

Anthony wasn't home anymore. He was still in Vietnam.

1 package (regular size box) lemon cake mix
4½oz (125g) whipped topping, such as Cool Whip
1 egg
½ cup (50g) powdered (icing) sugar

Grease cookie sheets (baking trays). Preheat oven to 350°F (180°C). Combine cake mix, whipped topping and egg in a large bowl. Stir until well mixed. Drop by teaspoon into sugar, roll to coat. Place 1–2 in (2.5–5cm) apart on cookie sheets. Bake 10–15 minutes. The cookies should be just turning golden over the whole surface.

Cardamom Shortbread

Tania in Sweden, in Stockholm after her solitary escape from the Soviet Union. What you are can't help but come out, even in Stockholm, after days and nights of being certain that you've been buried alive.

She used to sit at the Spivak Café and pretend to read the newspaper. After thirty minutes of staring at the same page, she would look up to find the afternoon waitress standing close with a pot of tea and a plate of wedges. Tatiana took, she ate.

The next day she would come back. Helga said nothing, but continued to bring Tatiana the tea and the sweetened cakes. Before she left Stockholm for good, in June of 1943, Tatiana came to Spivak one last time to say good-bye. "Helga," she asked. "What you giving me? What I eat?"

Helga smiled. "Cardamom shortbread. It's a Swedish delicacy."

Helga told Tatiana how to make it. Tatiana didn't write it down. Helga said, "You'll forget."

"I forget nothing," said Tatiana.

In New York she taught Vikki how to make the shortbread before she left for Germany. She taught Vikki because Anthony loved it and Tatiana wanted her boy to have something he loved to eat while she was possibly forever away. And so Vikki made it, and Anthony ate it, and because he was so young, he came to associate the cardamom shortbread not with his mother, but with Vikki, who, being Vikki, did nothing to dispel the illusion.

It was the one thing Vikki knew how to make (besides eggs).

Shortbread cookies with a bit of a glaze for extra sweetness. They were simple to make, which was why Vikki liked to make them, and they were addictive, which is why Anthony liked to eat them. She could have made them with almond extract, but Anthony, like his father, preferred lemon over almond, so that was how Vikki made it—the way Anthony liked it.

Cardamom Shortbread Cookies:

⅓ cup (65g) sugar
2 sticks (225g) butter, softened
2½ cups (320g) all-purpose (plain) flour
2–3 teaspoons ground cardamom
2 teaspoons vanilla extract
1 teaspoon lemon extract

Glaze:

1 cup (225g) powdered (icing) sugar
½ teaspoon vanilla extract
¼ teaspoon lemon extract
2–3 tablespoons milk

Preheat the oven to 350°F (180°C). Line two pie pans (glass or ceramic) with aluminum foil and spray with cooking oil. In the bowl of an electric mixer cream sugar and butter until light and fluffy. Spoon flour into measuring cup, fold into butter/sugar mix, stir in cardamom, vanilla, and lemon extract. Dough will be crumbly. Press into bottom of the pie pan, making it flat and thin, no more, no less than ⅛–¼ in (3–5mm) thick. Bake for 20–25 minutes until light golden. Cool in pan 10 minutes, then lift out by the foil. Leave on the foil and cut into 16 wedges while still warm, then carefully transfer the shortbread to a rack. Shortbread has a tendency to break. The longer it cools, the easier it will be to transfer.

For the glaze, in a small bowl mix powdered sugar, vanilla, lemon and milk. When the wedges have cooled slightly, drizzle glaze in long streaks over them.

Many years later, Tatiana and Vikki packed their bags and boarded a plane that took them 12,000 miles to Southeast Asia, to Saigon. In Saigon they were met by two lieutenant-majors of Military Assistance Command Vietnam (MACV) and escorted to Saigon Hospital—Vikki to collect the body of her husband, a colonel, and bring it back to the United States for burial, and Tatiana to attend to an injured son, a captain, and her gravely wounded Alexander, a major. Alexander was in the intensive care unit and in a coma. Tatiana was with him. Vikki, after spending half a day filling out paperwork, finally asked at the nurses' station where Anthony Barrington's room was.

She stood at his door for a few moments before she stepped in. He didn't see her, hadn't opened his eyes yet. It looked like he was sleeping. It was late afternoon, and the hospital room was sunny. Vikki could tell that Tatiana had already been in because Anthony had plants, a coffee-table book of Arizona wildflowers, and a blanket from home covering him.

Vikki entered, stood by him, then sat. Eventually he opened his eyes. They stared at each other in silence. Anthony was grievously injured, and her husband was dead. Anthony turned his face away. In a breaking voice, Vikki said, "I brought you something. Look." She lifted the foil off the small plate she was holding. On it, stacked like Legos, were cardamom shortbread cookies. She went around to stand by his good arm. Anthony reached up, took a cookie.

"Ah, good," he said. "Where'd you get these?"

"I made them."

"Back in the States? They're pretty fresh."

"No. Here. Your mother and I have a kitchen at the hotel."

"Where'd you get the cardamom?"

"Brought it with me."

Anthony was quiet. "Powdered sugar?"

"Brought it with me. I brought it all with me. I just needed an oven."

He ate another one. She set the plate on the table by his bed and sat down in a chair next to him.

Their mouths were all twisted.

"You look good," he said.

"You, too," she replied.

"Liar."

"Are you a liar?"

"No," said Anthony, blinking but not looking away this time. It was four and a half years since they had seen each other last. Now it was Vikki who couldn't bear to see him, shaking her gaze down onto his blanket, not wanting him to see the tears in her eyes, for herself, for her husband of twenty-two years, the husband who was dead because Anthony was alive, not wanting Anthony to see himself in her eyes, either.

"Does my mother know anything?" he asked, pausing. "I mean . . . about you and me?"

"If by anything, you mean everything, then yes."

Anthony put his one arm over his face. "God, Vikki."

"How could I have told them about your letter otherwise? How else could they have found you—or . . . Moon Lai?" Vikki groaned.

They fell mute.

"I'm sorry," said Anthony.

"Nothing to be sorry about, Ant," Vikki whispered back. She wiped her face.

"Oh, yes, there is." His arm reached for her. "Come here."

"Ant . . ."

"Vik, come here."

The nurse came in, the doctor.

"Ah, yes, Colonel Richter's wife," the doctor said, recognizing her. What he didn't say was, "Colonel Richter's widow." And that was probably best since, when they came in, Vikki was bent over Anthony, her wet face pressed flush to his face, and her eyes had been closed.

She stepped away from him. "I'll be back."

"Yes," said Anthony, squeezing her hand. "The shortbread will be gone next time I see you."

"I'll make more. I'll bring you more."

He held her hand for another moment, and then let go.

CHAPTER NINE

Psalms and Songs and Aykhal Visions

When all the world is old, lad,
And all the trees are brown;
And all the sport is stale, lad,
And all the wheels run down;
Creep home, and take your place there,
The spent and maimed among:
God grant you find one face there,
You loved when all was young.

Charles Kingsley

Sometimes, even as Tatiana grew older and the memories of the old life became fainter, she could still close her eyes and . . .

They pressed their bodies against the green building on Fifth Soviet.

She opened her eyes and was back home in Arizona, on her bed with the green and white bedspread and the large pillows. She sat on her window seat and looked out in the deep afternoon onto the Sonoran Desert and the McDowell Mountains and the Saguaro cacti painted with white flowers, shadowing the horizon . . . the blinding setting sun. Then she would close her eyes and . . .

They pressed their old bodies against the green building on Fifth Soviet.

"Mom, why didn't you ever teach Dad how to cook?"

They were gathered around her island on a late Saturday morning. All four children were home spending the weekend. Breakfast had already been served, and it was too early for lunch, but perhaps just right for elevenses: another cup of coffee with a snack from the fridge. Harry and Pasha settled on some ham with a brioche. Janie had her brioche with jam.

"Who says I didn't try?" said Tatiana.

"Oh, come on," said Harry. "You couldn't have tried that hard. My Amy wanted me to help with the kids' diapers. I said I didn't know how. I learned pretty quick, didn't I?"

"You think changing your sons diapers is the same as making *blinchiki?*"

"Changing diapers is much harder," Harry said, straight-faced.

He was shoved and pushed by his sister, he was laughed at by his brother. Alexander was at work so he couldn't be asked, but all the children said they would ask him that evening, and that evening at dinner they wanted to, but that evening Alexander was cooking. He made baked potatoes, a tenderloin, and corn on the cob, all on the grill, and he himself ladled out the strawberries and ice cream after dinner, while all Tatiana did was help him clean up afterward.

They sat outside on the covered porch, the music played through the speakers, the stars were out and the kids were in the pool. When the evening was perfect, it seemed churlish to ask why the father who carried weapons for ten years and scars on his body for the rest of his life, the father who crawled across thousands of miles to marry their mother and make one son, and then kept himself alive long enough for her to find him so that one day many years later they could give life to three more, why the father who brought the filet mignon to their table usually sat and was served at his wife's table, at their mother's table, at Tatiana's table.

Alexander's Ice Cream

There is no need for two metal bowls and rock salt and mixing by hand, when for a few dollars, he can buy a metal bowl that spins and in thirty minutes makes delicious soft-serve ice cream. But in Lazarevo, without electricity or Williams-Sonoma or a free market economy, in the middle of war, this kind of ice-cream maker proved difficult to acquire so Alexander had to make do with two metal bowls and rock salt. He had to become the ice-cream maker.

Imagine it first, then do it. In Lazarevo, they didn't grow tomatoes, and didn't make pastry, they had little flour, they had no meat, they ate what they grew and they grew what they could. They barely let the earth lie fallow, yet still . . .

An eighteen-year-old girl, newly married, was able to make for her soldier husband potato pancakes, and pancake batter, and even cabbage pie. They caught fish, and she made fish soup. There were no bananas, no plantains, no white bread, no canned goods aside from the Spam he brought with him, no sardines and no freezers. And yet the soldier man who had never cooked before imagined making something special for his child bride, something he knew she loved but hadn't had in a very long time. And so he, wishing to make her happy, wishing to do a small thing for her, imagined what he might need to do it. And in Lazarevo he went to a fishing plant and, using his Red Army credentials, using all the powers of persuasion at his disposal, including two bottles of vodka, two cans of Spam, and two hundred roubles, bartered for some rock salt, which the fishermen used to preserve fish, and a small amount of ice from a fish storage room.

From an old man too old to go to war, Alexander borrowed two metal buckets, one large, one small that fit inside the other, the small one two-thirds the size of the large, like a sublime Fibonacci frame. He picked some blueberries, he cleaned their stems. He didn't have lemon, but he managed to get a cup of sugar from the old ladies his bride had lived with. And he got one of them to help him get the cream that rose to the top of the fresh milk they got from the cows each morning. He macerated the blueberries with the sugar for half an hour, he added the cream, he placed these items into the small bucket. Into the large bucket he placed rock salt and ice. He set the small bucket inside the large one, and he mixed his blueberry cream, until the sides of the bucket got cold, until the mixture got icy, until it started to freeze and, as he was mixing it, to thicken. He stirred until the ice melted. It was slightly soft, but he did succeed in making his new wife ice cream in a small fishing village named Lazarevo. And when the wife saw it, she cried.

"Don't cry, eat. It'll melt," he said.

Things were a bit different fifty years down the pike, down the miles and years of a long, complicated life. Ice was abundant, refrigeration was in, rock salt was no longer necessary, there was plenty of lemon and blueberries and sugar and heavy cream. There was plenty.

Almost as if there was nothing else.

On the morning of their fiftieth wedding anniversary, before the renewal of their vows at Santa Maria's Church in Scottsdale, before the grand ballroom of the Arizona Biltmore Hotel was taken over by 400 guests for a day-long celebration, Alexander got up early while Tatiana was still sleeping and from the fridge got out two pints of strawberries.

Imagine it first, then do it.

Afterward he came back to bed and fell asleep.

In the bright morning, on the white sheets, covered with a large warm hunter-green down quilt, Tatiana stared at a sleeping Alexander until he woke up. "On the most important day of his life, the soldier sleeps till noon," she said softly.

"This is not the most important day of my life," said Alexander, jumping up. "And you know nothing."

They made the bed, began to get ready.

"I know what the children got us for our anniversary present," she said.

"So do I," said Alexander.

It was a two-week trip to St. Petersburg, Russia.

They stopped their ablutions and turned to each other. "Do you want to go?" he asked.

"I'll go if you want," she replied. They stopped speaking.

Alexander and Tatiana meandered off Nevsky, down the Griboyedov canal towards the Church of the Spilt Blood, then back to Nevsky to the Moika, past it, to the Arc of the General Staff, to the Winter Palace Square, to the Winter Palace, around the Winter Palace to the Neva, and then they walked down the granite carapace headed towards the unknown. On the opposite side of the river, the golden spire of Peter and Paul's cathedral blazed in the morning light.

"I can't do it," Tatiana said. "I can't walk down the streets of our life with you."

"I know." They turned back to their reflections in the mirror.

In front of their family, Alexander and Tatiana renewed their vows at the family church. She wore a crème silk dress with maroon shoes and a maroon hat. Tatiana, who still weighed what she weighed in 1943 (almost), who still had her blonde hair, her open smile, her faded freckles, stood small next to Alexander's big body in black tie.

"Shura, I can't believe what you look like," she whispered, gazing at him at the altar.

"What?" he said. "Old? Gray? Done for?" He took her hand and kissed it. "You're not going to be racked with doubt again, are you, while we're waiting for the priest?"

She chuckled softly. "I think it's too late for that. The kids are watching."

"Yes. Can't annul the marriage," said Alexander, "after it's been so thoroughly consummated."

"Shh!"

"I was talking about the children," he said calmly.

Tatiana tried to regain her composure. "What have you chosen to read?"

"What have *you* chosen to read?"

"From the Song of Solomon."

"Oh, no," said Alexander, moving closer to her. "In front of the *children?*"

She nearly laughed out loud in a church. "Now you."

He leaned in. "'Who can find a virtuous woman?'" he quoted quietly from Proverb thirty-one. "'For her price is far above rubies.'"

"Hmm," said Tatiana. "Have you tried diamonds?"

And Alexander did laugh out loud in a church.

Father John stepped forward to stand in front of them. He cleared his throat, his glittering eyes on the congregation and on Tatiana and Alexander. "Fifty years ago, these two people stood in front of another altar of God as they stand in front of us today, wanting to reaffirm that covenant. They have asked me to speak the same words the priest commenced with in 1942.

"Most gracious God," the priest began. "Look with favor upon

203

this man and this woman living in a world for which your Son gave His life. Make their life together a sign of Christ's love to this sinful and broken world. Defend this man and this woman from every *enemy*. Lead them into peace. Let their love for each other be a seal upon their hearts, a mantle upon their shoulders, and a crown upon their foreheads. Bless them in their work and in their friendship, in their sleeping and in their waking, in their joys and their sorrows, in their life, and in their death." Father John smiled. "Now turn to each other. You have prepared your own readings. Alexander?"

Alexander turned to Tatiana. "Who can find a virtuous woman?" he said in his deep voice, taking her hands. "For her price *is* far above rubies." He tried not to smile, and she tried not to smile. "Give strong drink unto him that is ready to perish. Let him drink and forget his poverty, and remember his misery no more. The heart of her husband does safely trust in her. She will do him good and not evil all the days of her life." He nodded. "She seeks wool and flax and she works willingly with her hands." Alexander squeezed Tatiana's hands. "She is like the merchants' ships. She brings her food from afar." Tatiana's eyes filled with tears. She shook her helpless head as if to stop him. "She rises while it is still night and gives meat to her household." Alexander's voice cracked. "She perceives that her merchandise is good. Her candle does not go out by night." He paused. "She is not afraid of the snow for her household: for all her household *are* clothed in scarlet. Her husband is known at the gates, when he sits among the elders of the land. She makes herself coverings of tapestry. Strength and honor *are* her clothing. She opens her mouth with wisdom; and in her tongue *is* the law of kindness. She eats not the bread of idleness. Her children rise up and call her blessed and her husband also, and he praises her," Alexander said. "Many daughters have done virtuously, but you have excelled them all. Give her the fruit of her hands; and let her own works praise her at the gates." He bowed his head momentarily. "Shh," he whispered to her, shaking slightly.

There was silence in the pews.

Father John turned to Tatiana.

She wiped her face. "The song of songs," Tatiana began, "which is Solomon's. Let him kiss me with the kisses of his mouth, for his love is better than wine. By night on my bed I sought him whom my soul loves, I sought him but I found him not. I will rise now and go about the city and the streets, and in the broad ways I will seek him whom my soul loves: I found him. I held him and would not let him go. My beloved spake, and said unto me, Rise up, my love, my fair one, and come away. For the winter is past, the rain is over and gone. The flowers appear on the earth, the time of singing of birds is come. My beloved is mine, and I am his, he feeds among the lilies. His head is as the most fine gold, his locks are black as raven. His eyes are as the eyes of doves by the rivers of waters. His cheeks are as a bed of spices, his lips like lilies. His hands are as gold rings set with beryl. His legs are as pillars of marble. His mouth is most sweet: he is altogether lovely. This is my beloved, and this is my friend." Alexander's eyes unblinkingly stared at Tatiana. "Set me as a seal upon your heart," she said. "As a seal upon your arm, for love is strong as death, the coals thereof are coals of fire, which has a most vehement flame." She blushed. "Many waters cannot quench love, neither the floods can drown it. Rise up, my love, my

fair one, and come away." She lowered her gaze, and stared at the
planked floor of the church.

They renewed and vowed and confirmed and kissed and danced to
the Anniversary Waltz in four languages and "*E Lucevan Le Stelle*"
in six renditions, they ate to bursting and spent all day and night
with their children, grandchildren and friends. There was music,
food and drink. There was plenty.

Almost as if there was nothing else.

"Tania?" They were in their bedroom. It was late, and they had
just come back. Alexander was still in his tux, the cummerbund off,
the bow tie now loosened.

"Yes, darling?" She had perched on the corner of the bed and
was bending to take off her shoes and stockings. "You hungry? I can
make you something. Though how you can eat after that—"

"What do you think you'd be doing now if you hadn't gone back
to Europe to find me?" He opened the French doors and lit a
cigarette, blowing smoke out into the night.

Tatiana straightened out. The shoes and stockings remained on.
"What?"

"Please. Tell me. How do you see it, your future, except without
me?"

"What are you talking about? Obviously I didn't see it. Don't see it."

"You almost didn't go back. You were so close to not going back.
Or you could've gone back and never found me. I could have been

too far gone for you to find me. You could have not come to Berlin. Not found Stepanov. Many, many things could have happened or not happened. Tell me. What would have been next for you?"

"Shura, please." Her hands tensed around her knees.

"No, Tania, you please. Tell me."

"Well, I don't know." She struggled with herself. "Why in the world do you want to talk about this now, today of all days?"

"Precisely because it is today of all days. Why are you equivocating?"

"I'm not equivocating." She paused. "What do you think would've happened to *you*?" she asked, equivocating. She lowered her eyes.

"Yes, don't look at me," he said. "As if I don't know what you're doing. Anyway, what was your question? What would've happened to *me*? Ah, that's easy. I would've been taken to Kolyma. I know what my sentence was. Twenty-five years. I would have stayed in prison for three years, five, ten, and then I would have tried to escape."

In a small voice she asked, "Tried, or escaped?" She kicked off her high heels. They were killing her feet. He watched her. *Watched her take off her high heels because they were killing her feet.* She nearly gave out. "Shura . . ." she breathed out, opening her hands to him.

"Tried. Or escaped," he said flatly, still near the French doors, one foot in, one out. "Either way, the result would have been the same. I would've been caught. Either I would have been shot dead or taken to Novaya Zemlya, to Lenin's Island, up in the Arctic Circle, where I would have spent until the mid-sixties wishing I had been shot dead."

"Alexander, please . . ."

But he continued. "In the sixties, when they were rehabilitating many old soldiers, I would have been 'pardoned' and released. I would have been sent to exile, to Magadan, or worse, to Aykhal."

"Aykhal? Where *is* that?"

"Precisely. There I would have mined the alluvial deposits for ten years or so. Until I was rehabilitated and in the seventies allowed to return to Leningrad. They would've reinstated my rank, perhaps even promoted me. They would have given me an exclusive membership at the Party athletic club, so I could swim in style any time I wanted to. Suspecting that I spoke flawless English, they would have given me a cushy position as a military advisor and my own apartment near Senate Square where I could look out my windows onto the statue of the Bronze Horseman. During the night I'd pull the curtains open to let the northern sun melt into the burning horizon and rise again behind the Neva."

"Have you given this much thought, Alexander?" Tatiana said, her sad voice tinged with bitterness.

He said nothing, silently sad and bitter back.

"Why? Why torture yourself?" Why torture yourself *today* is what she wanted to add.

"And you?"

"I don't think about *this*."

"Not this, no. But tell me what you would have done if you hadn't gone looking for me? Many people, I'm sure, judged you harshly for leaving our son."

"Yes," was all she said. But she still didn't answer him.

He sighed in exasperation. "Would you have married Edward Ludlow?"

"I don't know. Possibly. Wouldn't *you* have married again?"

"No," said Alexander. "How could I have, Tatiana? I was already married."

"Shura, God!" She nearly covered her face. "Please don't do this."

"So you would have married Edward. Would you have stayed in New York?"

"Probably. I may have eventually come here, settled here." Her voice was low.

"Had other children?"

"Probably." This was said in an inaudible whisper. "Though seeing what it took even for us, the answer should be possibly, not probably."

"You're wrong. It's because it was you and me that it took so long." Alexander fell quiet.

"Ah, finally even you are reconsidering this conversation," said Tatiana.

"No," he said, but didn't say much more. "Anthony would have been safe. He wouldn't have gone to Vietnam."

With a closing heart, Tatiana shook her head. "Oh yes, he would have. He would've wanted to be like the warrior father he never knew." She swallowed to wet her dry throat. "He would have come back, and he might have even been injured. He would have still moved up in rank, he would have become Chairman of the Joint Chiefs. And as Communism was falling like bricks in the Berlin Wall, he would have gone back to Russia, just as he did a few years ago to talk the Soviet government into releasing the records on the U.S. servicemen MIA since the Second World War. He would have asked me to go with him. And I would have gone."

"You would've gone to Russia?"

"To find you? Yes. For you, I would have gone back to Russia."

Alexander stepped inside the bedroom.

"And we would have found you."

"You think?" he asked. His voice trembled.

"Absolutely."

"What makes you so sure?"

"I'm positive. We would have."

He came to sit beside her on the bed. "How old would I be when you found me?"

She looked at him. "Seventy-three. Like now."

He looked at her. "And you sixty-eight."

"Yes."

"We would not have seen each other for fifty years."

"Yes."

"Where is Edward?"

"Passed on years ago. He was fifteen years older than me. He died in 1985."

They stared at each other. A small tear ran down Tatiana's face.

Grand Hotel Europe, June, 1991

When forty-eight-year-old Anthony walked into the ballroom and restaurant at the Grand European Hotel, his staff of two and the four Russian generals were already sitting at the table. Anthony was forty minutes late for an hour-long meeting to review his speech for Soviet television that evening. He came to the table, apologized, and sat between his assistant and his aide. Anthony's contact, General Vennikov and three other Soviet generals deep into their sixties, were sitting across from him at the rectangular table in the back by the stage, sipping tea and reading *Izvestiya*.

"Can we begin?" asked Anthony.

Turned out they had already begun. The Soviets had made a number of changes to the speech, and as Anthony watched, a number more. One of the generals, in between endless cigarettes, was crossing out with spectacular glee practically every other word, another was busy pouring himself vodka, and the third was chatting up the waitress.

Vennikov eyed the heavily revised speech with satisfaction, *such* satisfaction that Anthony said to him, "Why don't you just have your generals write my speech for me? Perhaps that's what I need. Four speechwriters."

Studying Anthony, the smoking general smoked down another half a cigarette before he exhaled. Anthony shook his head. The man was not coughing. He *was* smiling, however. He said in English, "I would offer you a cigarette but I can see by your slightly irritated American manner that you don't smoke."

"I do smoke, and it's not the smoking that's irritating me," said Anthony.

Vennikov said in his heavily accented English, "When we're in your country, you can revise our speeches all you want General Ludloff, but until then . . ."

"It's not the revising, it's the re-writing," Anthony broke in. "And it's General *Ludlow*. All right, let's see it. Let's get it over with."

"You can keep your speech as you like, General Ludlow," said the smoker, "since it's in English. But since I'm your translator, permit me to read it how I like in Russian. I am not arguing with you about your speech. I am just saying, a lecture is perhaps *not* what we need."

The translator's English was much better than Vennikov's. He knew his job well. Anthony was impressed. The changes he had made to the speech in his translation were informed changes, geared mainly to diplomacy and tact, rather than toward a blatant manipulation of facts. He was versed in the MIA situation and had a careful way of presenting the salient facts to the Soviet government. His red pen in hand and a cigarette in his mouth, the translator said, "General Ludlow, have you ever thought of learning Russian? In your line of work it would come in quite handy."

"Thank you for your unsolicited advice, General. I do not write in Russian. But I do speak Russian. And read Russian. Which is how I am aware of the changes you are making in your, shall we say, quite loose interpretation of my speech."

Vennikov said, "The problem with your speech is that you are wrong about us, General Ludloff; we just need a little time. We cannot repair everything in a month. We are working hard on the MIA problem. We are improving our current identity records. In Afghanistan we know the names of nearly all the dead and wounded Soviet soldiers," he added proudly.

"And more to the point," said the translator, "your comments about the difference between the Soviets and the Americans are inflammatory." The translator read from Anthony's speech. "'Our president wrote a letter to his children before the Iraqi war a few months ago and in it said, 'How many American boys am I willing to sacrifice to win this? And the answer is, not one. Not a single one. One is too many.'" He exhaled smoke rings at Anthony. "Maybe we could stop there. Do we really need to add that we in the Soviet Union thought twenty million was not enough?"

Anthony studied him with surprise. "I didn't write that in my speech," he exclaimed.

"No?" said the translator, his eyes twinkling. He turned back to the text. "Must be my mistake, then. My English isn't what it used to be." He picked up his red pen.

Amused, Anthony exchanged a look with his aide.

The translator lit another cigarette. "You had some MIA problems in Vietnam, didn't you?"

"Yes. Unsolvable problems so far. The Vietnamese refuse to cooperate." Anthony shrugged. "A thousand MIAs. We'll get them. Slowly but surely, we'll get them."

Nodding, the translator said, "I am sure you will, General Ludlow. After all, here you are, *fifty* years after the Second World War, returning to recover information on a mere ninety-one American soldiers missing in action."

"Actually," said Anthony, "just one."

The waitress brought them vodka, seven shot glasses, and Russian hors d'ouvres. Caviar, black bread, white bread, butter, herring, salami. A little salad Olivier, a little venigret. They broke for recess.

Anthony liked the Russian cuisine, taking some bread and caviar and herring. It was his Russian blood. He drank a shot of vodka in the middle of the afternoon as if he had done it all his life. He raised a glass to the newly forged relationship between the Soviets and the Americans, downed two full shots of vodka for this special friendship and ate the venigret and salad Olivier with gusto. The generals watched Anthony with curiosity. The translator said, "You drink like a true Russian."

"Yes," said Anthony. "Must be my Russian blood."

"Oh, who is Russian in your family?"

"My mother."

"Really?" said the translator. "American-born?"

"Soviet-born," said Anthony, with his usual diplomacy.

Vennikov gasped. "Your mother was born in the *Soviet Union?*" The generals stared at Anthony now with more than idle curiosity. Anthony was delighted.

His assistant nudged him under the table. "General Ludlow, may I have a quick word with you, sir?" They stood up and stepped away a few feet. "Sir, we might want to be careful with the information we give to these people."

"Why, Dave?" Anthony asked lightly. "You don't think we're safe?"

"Who the hell knows? Six months ago they were abducting their own leader and holding him hostage at a holiday resort! These Soviets are an unknown quantity. We must be more careful."

Anthony made a serious face. "You're right. I don't want to cause an international incident. As the general points out, we're not here to inflame. Or are we?"

They went back to the table. Vennikov asked if everything was all right.

"It's great," said Anthony. "Where were we? I think we were discussing point thirteen, dealing with the immediate notification and discourse between the two countries regarding any new information on war prisoners or missing in action."

"General Ludlow," said Vennikov, "frankly I'm surprised to hear your mother is from the Soviet Union. This changes things. Yesterday, with you present, I showed her our war records. I was being courteous, a good host. I thought she was looking for someone out of idle curiosity."

"With all due respect, General," said Anthony, "did you think my mother came here from the United States to look for someone just because she was idly curious? My mother doesn't have time to be idly curious. The President of the United States offered her the chair of the American Red Cross. She told him she was too busy to accept. She is not here on vacation."

"What was she looking for?" asked the translator.

"She was trying to find the name of a man in the war records who had been thought dead since 1943."

"Why does she think he is dead?" asked Vennikov.

"She has his death certificate."

Vennikov laughed out loud. He shook his head. "General Ludloff, if she has his death certificate, I'd say he is more than *thought* dead."

"That's what *she* thought," said Anthony. "But why does his name not appear in the death records then, not here, nor in Moscow?"

"I told you," Vennikov said cheerfully, "our records are far from complete."

"I can see that." Anthony was growing impatient. "But broadly speaking, were death certificates issued for soldiers who were still alive?"

Vennikov shrugged. "I suppose not. What's her interest in him, anyway?"

"He was her husband," replied Anthony without further ado.

Stony silence fell at the table. The Soviet men stared at Anthony with slack confusion.

Dave, the assistant, shot up from the table and said, "General, could I see you for a—"

"No, David. Sit back down."

David sat back down.

Anthony smiled. His mother would be proud of him. Vennikov was red in the face. The other two generals took their cues from Vennikov.

It was the translator who puzzled Anthony, however. His strong-jawed face was not slack, nor was it dumbstruck, and his mouth wasn't open. His eyes remained unblinkingly on Anthony, as he cleared his throat and said, "General Ludlow, what was the name of the dead officer?"

"Alexander Belov, I think," replied Anthony.

There was a short silence at the table followed by raucous laughter from three Russian men, three *excluding* the translator who stared intensely at Anthony. Anthony blinked momentarily, and saw a flicker of —

Vennikov, still laughing, said, "Your mother should have just asked *me*. I would have helped her immediately. She could have saved herself and me a lot of aggravation." He stuck his finger out at the translator. "*This* is General Alexander Below. As you can see for yourself *he* is not dead. He did serve in our great war, proudly and well, and is a many times decorated officer in the *Red* Army. Bring your mother here. Maybe this is the man she is looking for. Maybe this is her dead husband!" He did not stop laughing, and neither did the other two generals. Anthony's assistant and aide smiled nervously.

Only Anthony and the translator stared mutely at each other.

"I am probably wrong," muttered Anthony, lowering his gaze. "There must be so many Alexander Belovs. It's quite a common name, no?" He raised his eyes again.

"Perhaps," agreed the translator non-committally. "What is *your* full name, General?"

"Anthony Ludlow," replied Anthony.

"Your *full* name."

"Anthony Alexander Barrington Ludlow," replied Anthony, and saw the translator's face grow white. A film clouded his raw, unwavering eyes.

Vennikov said, "General Belov, you can thank your lucky stars it is not *you* that woman is looking for."

"Not for many years now—fifty-five to be exact," said the translator, "but once upon a time, Alexander Barrington *was* the name I carried."

David, a grown man, was whimpering. "General Ludlow, this is a public relations disaster. Please, could we talk a moment?"

"No," snapped Anthony, without taking his eyes off the man across the table. Neither Anthony nor the translator spoke. He could not look away from Alexander. "She remarried," he said in English. "She thought you were—"

"I know what she thought," Alexander interrupted. "She still has the death certificate." His hands shook as he tried to light a cigarette. Finally he lit it, inhaled deeply, smoked it down, stubbed it out and lit another.

Anthony looked at the translator's hands and then at his own. They were the same hands. His were palms down on the table.

217

Anthony could no longer raise his eyes.

Vennikov came to the rescue. "General Belov, this must be an administrative error, don't you agree? Why would there be a death certificate filled out with your name? It's a different Alexander Belov."

The translator stood up.

Anthony remained sitting. His legs were not to be trusted.

Vennikov exclaimed, "You're not the same Alexander Belov, I tell you!" He spun to Alexander. "General Belov, if you're the man she is looking for, that means that General Ludloff is your—"

"Son," Alexander finished. "It means that General Anthony Ludlow is my son."

Swallowing the lump in his throat, Anthony stood up tall and straight.

Disgruntled, Vennikov looked at Alexander. "This is impossible!" he growled.

Alexander stepped away from the table and said, "Haven't you heard the nasty rumors about me, Comrade Vennikov?"

"I didn't believe them. I thought they were vicious lies."

Alexander turned to Anthony.

Anthony brought his trembling hand to his temple and saluted the man standing in front of him.

Alexander saluted his son back. He blinked.

Anthony's hand remained frozen at his temple.

"Where is your mother?" asked Alexander.

"And so, you see?" said Tatiana quietly. "Here we would be. You and me."

Now it was Alexander's turn to stare at her dumbstruck. "Indeed, Tania. I thought you never thought about it?"

"Oh, once or twice. And here we would still be, just like now," she whispered.

"Except everything would be different."

Their souls, from her eyes to his, flew back and forth. "Not everything," said Tatiana, closing her eyes. Thirty feet in front of her, in full military uniform with black hair underneath his beige cap with the red star, stood Alexander.

And Alexander closed his. Barefoot in a yellow sundress with her hair in two little braids, on her tiptoes on top of his boots stood Tatiana.

Back then, when they closed their eyes, they could not imagine a life without one another. Alexander went to Lazarevo because he could not imagine it.

Tatiana went to Germany because she could not imagine it.

With bowed heads they retreated, busied themselves with their nighttime routine, with getting ready for bed. They tried to make small talk. "You know, you never did learn to cook that beef *pho* from Vietnam. I loved that stuff," he said.

"Yeah, well . . ." she averred.

And he averted his eyes. "We can always get some at Phuong's." Phuong's was a Vietnamese restaurant in Scottsdale.

"That's a good idea," Tatiana said vaguely. She had never gone and never intended to.

And they moved on, talking about other things, making life from other things.

"Shura, want to hear a joke?"

"Love to."

"An Englishman, a Frenchman and a Russian are looking at a painting of Adam and Eve. The Englishman says, *look how stoic, how poised. They must be English.* And the Frenchman says, *Nonsense, look at how erotic, how sensual, how full of flesh. They must be French.* And the Russian says, *Absolutely not. They're naked, they have no food, no water, and no shelter, yet they're told they have everything. They're Russian.*"

First he laughed.

And then he whispered, "Wait, I'll be right back." When he returned, he was holding a small bowl in his hands. She sat up. He sat at the edge of the bed, she closed her eyes, and he gave her a taste of something he had made earlier that morning.

"You made me *ice cream?*" Tatiana said, stunned.

"Well, it is our fiftieth wedding anniversary. If not now, when?"

Strawberry Ice Cream

2 cups (350g) fresh, ripe, thinly sliced strawberries

¼ cup (55ml) fresh lemon juice

1 cup (200g) sugar, divided in halves

¼ cup (55ml) orange liqueur

1 cup (225ml) milk

2 cups (450g) heavy cream

1 teaspoon vanilla extract

First macerate the strawberries. In a medium stainless steel bowl, place straberries, lemon juice, ½ cup (100g) sugar, and orange liqueur. Stir gently to coat strawberries, cover and let stand for two hours.

Strain the strawberries, reserving the juice. Mash or purée ¾ of the strawberries, reserving the rest.

In a medium bowl, combine milk and the remaining ½ cup (100g) sugar, beating with a hand mixer until sugar is dissolved, a minute or two.

Add puréed strawberries, the reserved strawberry juice, heavy cream and vanilla and mix with hand mixer until blended.

Place in the frozen bowl of an ice-cream maker and churn for about 20–25 minutes until mixture turns thick and frozen. In the last five minutes of churning, add the remaining ¼ of the strawberries. Eat soft-serve, or place in a freezer-safe container.

She ate it and cried. Soon he put the melting ice cream away. "Shura," Tatiana whispered, darling, forget what should have been. Remember all that was."

"Tatiasha, babe," Alexander whispered, coming back to bed to be covered, "my one and only wife, forget our age, our splendid youth, forget it all and let our crazy love make us young."

Index